DEATH IN A DECK CHAIR

DEATH
IN A DECK CHAIR

by K. K. Beck

WALKER AND COMPANY
NEW YORK

This edition printed in 1985.

First published in the United States of America
in 1984 by the Walker Publishing Company, Inc.

Published simultaneously in Canada by John Wiley & Sons
Canada, Limited, Rexdale, Ontario.

Library of Congress Cataloging in Publication Data

Beck, K. K.
    Death in a deck chair.

    I. Title.
PS3552.E248D4   1984   813'.54   84-19491
ISBN 0-8027-5601-8

Book design by Teresa M. Carboni

Printed in the United States of America

10 9 8 7 6 5 4 3 2

for Aunt Gudrun who loved a cozy murder

CHAPTER ONE

*T*hat day in August when we boarded the *Irenia* in South-
ampton for our journey home was damp and miserable. The
confetti clung wetly to the deck, the colors running in pastel
rivulets. The horns and noisemakers sounded a valiant but
feeble note against the wind. I tucked my sodden handkerchief back into my pocket. It seemed useless to wave the
damp clump at the receding figures of my English cousins
on the dock. They formed a little knot of tweed coats, with
pink-cheeked smudges for faces. It was fitting, I thought,
that the weather at the end of our travels should mirror my
own sense of letdown. Our trip around the world might well
be the last adventure I'd ever have. Perhaps, as an old lady,
I'd take my souvenirs and sketchbooks out of lavender-
scented paper and display them wistfully, trying to summon
back to memory the sounds and sights and smells of all the
places I'd visited. I sighed at this grim prospect. In the
autumn I'd be off to college, and then, who knows, perhaps I
would marry. I sighed once more.

Of course, I thought harshly, the fact that this trip had
been the one episode of excitement in my life was my own
fault. If I'd been truly plucky, I'd have come up with some
adventurous mode of life, perhaps as an aviatrix. I saw
myself tucking my curls beneath a leather helmet, one
booted foot delicately poised on the airplane, adjusting
goggles, smiling broadly, and giving a sweeping wave before
swinging into the cockpit. But I didn't think I really wanted
to be an aviatrix, or a missionary in Africa like my cousin
Maggie, who sent us pictures of herself in acres of white

7

gauze, her small, pinched face peering out from underneath a pith helmet. I didn't even want to be an actress. I leaned against the rail, the damp mist cooling my face, closed my eyes tightly, and wished as hard as I could for adventure.

Which, I reflected a second later, was probably a very foolish, and perhaps even dangerous, thing to do. I opened my eyes again and tried to push these strange yearnings to the back of my mind.

But I was still a little wistful, restless, and even impatient with dear Aunt Hermione. She fussed so as we arranged ourselves in our cabin. It was a cozy little cabin, but altogether unnautical, with chintzes and soft carpet underfoot, a pair of beds you couldn't really call bunks, a slipper chair in moiré silk, and a pale wood dressing table with a large oval mirror.

"Quite luxurious, really," said Aunt Hermione. "Somehow I expected a British ship to be a little more Spartan."

She sat heavily on one of the beds, and pronounced it "quite firm and nice. I *do* hope the food turns out as well as our cabin. You know, one is quite *trapped* aboard ship. If the food's not very good, there it is. You have to eat it." She sighed.

I went to the dressing table and began to extract damp confetti from my hair. I watched my aunt in the mirror as she peeled off gray suede gloves. "Now my dear," she said briskly, "we are all installed. I've spoken to the deck steward, and we have some very nice deck chairs on the port side. It *is* the port side we're supposed to want going west, isn't it? And the dining steward has arranged a perfectly nice table at the second sitting. The cabin steward is going to bring a vase for those lovely irises."

I cast my eye over an armful of flowers twisted in wet tissue paper. They were the kind of irises with fuzzy beards on them, and yellow centers. I much preferred the smaller, neater ones, in deep violet.

"Very gallant of our cousin Basil to bring us irises in

honor of your name, don't you think? Especially as they're out of season. He certainly seemed fond of you, my dear."

"Yes," I replied abstractly, frowning over a beribboned basket in front of me on the dresser. "He proposed just as we got on the boat train. Why do people want to give us all this fruit? It's not as though we'll get scurvy in a week's crossing." I removed the basket, which contained pears, from the dresser, and put it on top of my steamer trunk.

Aunt Hermione began to fiddle with the heads and tails of her furs. She never could remember which set of jaws undid the entire arrangement. "Do help me with this, will you, Iris? And why not put the pears in that corner, with the oranges. Those oranges look like the peculiar red ones we had in Spain. I really don't care for them at all. When I get home, I plan to eat a dozen good California oranges. Tell me, dear, did you let him down gently? Cousin Basil, I mean? I know he has a terribly weak chin, but he seemed like a pleasant young man."

"I don't think his proposal was a very serious one," I said, sorting through the pelts that embraced Aunt Hermione's stout figure. "He took my refusal very cheerfully, almost as if he were relieved. I imagine he proposes to some hapless female at least once a week." I released Aunt Hermione from her garland of small animals.

"Ah, thank you, dear." She shook the last of the rain from the fur. "Tell me, I've been meaning to ask you, did you form any sort of attachment to that young man with the ukulele we met on the *President Cleveland* going out to Pago Pago?"

I wrinkled my nose. "That college boy? No, not at all. He was nice enough, I suppose." Aunt Hermione had struck a nerve. I had rather imagined that somewhere in all the hotel lobbies and ship's dining rooms I might have found a suitable object for my affections. Just for a while, anyway. And I had met more young men than I had in the previous nineteen years. But I hadn't met anyone special. Instead, I had danced with innumerable pleasant young men at thé dansants, and chatted with them about nothing of importance. It had been thrilling when the matador in Madrid presented me with the ears, but I'd been unnerved when he presented himself at the Hotel Excelsior, and relieved that Aunt Hermione had had him ejected.

"You're so young and attractive," she said now, "and I shouldn't keep you all to myself. You've been so helpful and attentive on this trip, but I worry that you miss the companionship of people your own age. Let us hope there are some nice young people aboard the *Irenia*." She said this last with her characteristic confidence that hoping for something pleasant would make it so. We changed places, with the deftness borne of long practice in small hotel rooms and staterooms. She seated herself before the dressing table mirror; I flopped down on the bed and stretched out comfortably, while Aunt Hermione removed her gray cloche hat with a rather startling dove's wing that made her look a little like a lopsided Mercury. She examined her blue marcelled coiffure critically.

"Why don't you look through the passenger list and see if there's anyone interesting on board, while I see what I can do with this hair of mine. And perhaps we should ring for the steward again. You do want those flowers in water, don't you?"

I shrugged. "They're the hardy kind," I said. "And I imagine the steward is busy getting everyone vases. Let's wait a little longer."

"You mustn't be reluctant to ring for the steward," said my aunt. "That's his job, to fetch things. Shall we send for some sherry, too?" Aunt Hermione sighed. "I shall miss my afternoon sherry when we get back home. That horrid bootlegger of your father's *can't* seem to get ahold of a nice sherry at *any* price."

I kicked off my shoes and began to scan the passenger list. "Let's see . . . Abbot, Ashcroft, Beaulieu. . . . Aunt Hermione"—I caught her reflection in the glass—"I've had a wonderful time. Thank you so much for taking me. I can't think of anyone I'd rather travel with. We've seen so much, and done so many wonderful things. And I'll have plenty of time to be with people my own age when I start college in the fall."

"Iris dear, you are sweet," she answered. "It *has* been thrilling, hasn't it?"

I continued my perusal of the passenger list. "There is a count. A French one. And ooh, guess who's sailing with us? *Vera Nadi.*"

"That silly screen vamp? The one with the kohl-rimmed eyes?"

"They all have kohl-rimmed eyes. It must be. Who else would be named Vera Nadi?"

"I suppose you're right. I'm surprised she isn't on one of the more glamorous ships, like that new *Île de France*. Ridiculous name, to my mind . . . Vera Nadi, I mean. Not the *Île de France*. Will these pearls do? Help me with this clasp, will you?" I hooked the necklace while Aunt Hermione dusted her dear, round face with a little powder. I looked over her shoulder at my reflection, and tried to imagine my hazel eyes outlined with smudges of kohl.

If there were any nice young people aboard the *Irenia*, they weren't at our table. A middle-aged man with a strange, soft beard introduced himself as Professor Ignacz Probris- low. "And this is my secretary, Mr. Twist." He indicated a shy-looking young man with overbrilliantined hair and pale blue eyes. Mr. Twist's unexpectedly broad smile revealed a mouthful of crooked teeth.

"And Cardinal DeLaurenti," continued the professor with a Slavic lilt. The cardinal nodded and smiled.

"His eminence doesn't speak a word of English," muttered the man next to us, an Englishman with thinning hair and a pepper-and-salt moustache. He gestured obliquely to the cardinal. "Colonel Marris," he added with a nod, and dove into his dinner.

We looked for the captain, but his table was empty. Aunt Hermione's gentle inquiry as to his whereabouts elicited the news from the steward that he was on the bridge. "We're expecting a bit of rough weather," he added, and my aunt shuddered.

"Don't worry," I said cheerfully. "He's probably one of those unsociable captains. Any excuse to avoid the passengers."

Aunt Hermione frowned. She took a passionate interest in gold braid and was forever assaulting the captains of ships with questions about seamanship, the life of a seagoing man, and the possibility of encountering icebergs.

"Say, are you folks American?" a voice boomed to us from the next table over the quiet murmurs of the passengers and the gentle clink of china and cutlery. Warily, we turned and nodded.

"Judge Omar Griffin. And this is Mrs. Griffin. Lewiston, Idaho. Maybe we can get our tables changed and eat with you. I'm afraid we don't speak their lingo." He pointed with his knife at a slim dark couple across from him. They tried not to look alarmed at his outstretched knife, and spoke quietly to each other in French.

"Don't point, Omar," said Mrs. Griffin.

"I knew you were American because you switched your fork back," continued the judge. He demonstrated, setting his knife elaborately down and changing his fork to the other hand. The French couple giggled.

"Never understood that at all," said Colonel Marris. "Doesn't allow a man to smash things together. Waste of time, too." As if to prove a point, he heaped mashed potatoes, green beans, and roast beef together on the back of his fork, and gave it a swirl in his gravy.

"There is an interesting little story about that from the

war," said the professor, gamely attempting to start some sort of general conversation. "A group of German soldiers, entering an inn in Alsace, found a man, by all appearances an Alsatian peasant, in his blue smock. But he switched his fork back, and was of course arrested immediately, for he was an American. Summarily shot." The professor smiled at everyone, and the cardinal smiled back, apparently without comprehension.

"Alsace, you say?" said the colonel. "Thought it happened in Schleswig-Holstein."

"Hardly an amusing anecdote to the family of that boy," said Aunt Hermione sharply.

I sighed. I really didn't like to hear my elders relive the Great War. I remembered only knitting interminable pairs of socks and helmet liners at school. Miss Laurence, my teacher, had slapped my hand for pulling the yarn through with my needle instead of wrapping it with my hand. "That's the German way," she had said. But, of course, everybody had said her name was really Lorenz, and that she was over-zealous in trying to establish the proper patriotic tone.

"I didn't mean to offend, madame," replied the professor. "The peoples of many nations have suffered. I, who come from a once-proud nation that has disappeared entirely from the map of Europe, I, too, have suffered."

Aunt Hermione looked flustered. She had probably pegged the professor as a German. In spite of our extensive travels, she was vague about foreigners.

Mr. Twist tried to smooth things over. "I say, I *am* glad you're at our table. I've never been to America, and I'm awfully keen on hearing all about it."

Aunt Hermione told Mr. Twist of the mighty forests of Oregon, of the vastness of the Columbia River, of the bustle and vitality of Portland.

Coffee was handed round, and I watched the orchestra. "Sounds like a jazz band to me," harrumphed the colonel. "And not a proper ship's orchestra."

"And in America," continued Aunt Hermione with conviction, "it doesn't matter what your father did for a living. You have the same chance everyone else has. If you're eager to work..."

I gazed casually at the orchestra's piano player. I admired his dark, handsome face, his aquiline features, and he smiled at me.

Annoyed, I turned quickly to my left, and encountered the smiling face of the cardinal. The piano player's smile had been so smug and knowing, just this side of a leer, really, that I decided he must be very vain about his looks.

"Do you like sea voyages?" I asked the cleric above the din of a fox-trot. I didn't know much about Roman Catholics, and I hoped cardinals were allowed to talk to young women.

His eminence indicated in broken English that he spoke Italian and some French.

"Est-ce que vous aimez les voyages de mer?" I asked inanely.

When the fox-trot subsided, Mr. Twist extricated himself from Aunt Hermione's description of life in a democracy and asked me to dance. Once he had launched us into a credible two-step, he began to talk. I tried not to mind his damp palms.

"This is my first trip abroad," he said. "I'm quite thrilled. I never imagined I'd be able to travel, but, quite by chance, I obtained this post with the professor."

"How nice for you. What will you be doing for him?"

"Well, I'm not really certain. I shall begin when we arrive in Montreal. The professor is on a lecture tour."

"Aunt Hermione goes to lots of lectures. What's the professor's subject?"

" 'The Mind of the Criminal Lunatic,' he calls it. Fancy doing the same lecture over and over again! We're going to New York, even out west to Chicago. But then you live even farther west, so your aunt tells me. Out at the very edge."

"You'll love traveling, Mr. Twist. My aunt and I have been all around the world. It's been grand."

"You American women are so plucky," he said. And then, as if he'd been too familiar, he switched the subject. "Yes, I was fortunate to obtain the post. My vicar in the little village where I grew up recommended me. I had been working in a library. It was decent of the vicar to recommend me. I was a handful as a child. Beaned the choir mistress with the Book of Common Prayer once. But he remembered me. Even though my family is all gone, and I'd left the village."

I tried to imagine Mr. Twist hurling a prayer book, and failed. Still, I thought, he must have some spirit to him, after all.

Mr. Twist began to lose his precarious rhythm. The ship had rolled heavily and thrown us off a little, and then suddenly the orchestra sounded different. The piano was missing.

The piano player approached us, tapped Mr. Twist on the shoulder, and smiled at me. I appealed silently to Mr. Twist not to acquiesce, but to my chagrin, he withdrew. The pianist took me in his arms.

I was terribly annoyed that my new partner had caught my appraising glance earlier. I fixed my gaze over his shoulder and assumed as blasé an expression as I could muster.

"Come now, don't look so icy," he said. "Surely you welcome a rescue from that rabbity fellow? I dance to the music, while he had developed a very clever sort of counterpoint of his own."

It was true that although the two men were of the same general size and shape, the pianist was a much better dancer.

"I don't like cutting in," I said. And because this sounded priggish, I elaborated. "That is, I feel like some sort of slave at auction when just anyone can come and waltz away with me. It annoys me. And then it's so awkward for poor Mr.

Twist. He has to struggle back to the table through all these dancers."

"Twist," said my partner. "What an incredible name. Old pal of yours?"

"No, I just met him."

"He isn't by any chance traveling with the bearded fellow, is he?"

"Yes. Why do you ask?"

"Just investigating the competition," he said airily. "After all, we're all shut up together for a week and a half. Can't have the best-looking girl on board throw herself away on Mr. Twist. I'd watch it, my dear. He'll be cornering you on the promenade deck, pressing you into endless games of shuffleboard and deck tennis, gazing moodily out over the rail and telling you your eyes are like the sea. I've seen it happen a dozen times. Sea voyages give these fellows like Twist more courage than they'll ever have again."

"I think you've got your nerve," I said coolly. "Mr. Twist is simply an amiable young man, all excited about his first trip. You mustn't be so cruel as to chide people for being awkward. After all, we can't all be as charming as you imagine yourself to be."

"True, true. Actually, your eyes aren't like the sea at all; they're . . . let's see . . ."

"They're beautiful when they're angry," I snapped, inwardly cursing the fellow for being so attractive.

"Right. Now, let's give your mother over there, with the lorgnette fixed in our direction—"

"My aunt."

"Well, your aunt, then, let's give her a turn and duck behind these palms into a dimly lit corner of the saloon."

"My aunt is certainly not as interested in our progress as your boss is," I replied. The orchestra leader was gesturing madly with his elbows toward my partner while trying to conduct. A jagged tuba line ran through the music, the result of an unsuccessful effort to cover for the piano.

He shrugged. "This is my last crossing with this outfit anyway. Then I'm on to Chicago to really learn about jazz. No more of this watered-down hotel-lobby music for me. Ah, but here we are, obscured by foliage."

"I suppose this cheap stuff works for you every time," I said. "Naive young girls panting for shipboard romance, and all that."

"You've got it all wrong," he said nonchalantly. "It must be true love this time. My specialty so far has been the more mature type. You know, hungry eyes and little lapdogs."

"Are you ever serious?" I asked.

"Yes I am," he said, and caught my wrist in his hand. "Stay away from Twist. You could be in danger."

I laughed. But I was secretly a little frightened.

"No, I don't mean from an amorous piano player. There is a real possibility of danger. I can't tell you any more."

"You're mad," I exclaimed. "And you're hurting my wrist."

His face softened. "I'm sorry. Perhaps I am mad. *But watch out for Twist.*"

"Iris, dear," said Aunt Hermione, when I had been returned to our table. "I do think cutting in is an abominable custom. I mean, the musicians aren't supposed to dance with the passengers anyway, are they?" She seemed slightly dubious on this point. Aunt Hermione was a terrible chaperone. "You *will* join us for bridge, won't you, dear? The colonel and the professor and I are looking for a fourth. Mr. Twist"—she frowned—"does not play bridge."

We repaired to the smoking room, a dark, wood-paneled room with comfortable clusters of sofas and chairs, green baize tables, a large mahogany bar, and a cheerful fire. It smelled of cigars, furniture polish, and brandy.

"When in doubt, I always bid no trump," said Aunt Hermione as I put down my hand. "Oh well, I suppose you *tried* to warn me when you kept insisting on clubs." She sighed.

"Please try not to review the bidding until the hand has been played," I said firmly. The colonel shot me a grateful glance.

I couldn't stand to witness the shambles that was sure to result from Aunt Hermione's erratic bidding, so I decided to spend my time as dummy elsewhere.

I walked among the tables and chairs, playing my favorite shipboard game: trying to match the names on the passenger list with the faces on board. I was thrilled to discover, by the light of a green-shaded lamp, the famous face of Vera Nadi. She was a gaunt beauty, with large black eyes and a chiseled crimson mouth. Her hair was wrapped in jade green silk, and she wore a black crepe de chine gown that revealed ivory shoulders.

Her contralto tones drifted across the murmurs of conversation. "An interview cannot be arranged. You must not bother me in a public room. Please leave me."

Judge Griffin played bridge at a nearby table. "Say, Louise, that's Vera Nadi. The moving picture star," he whispered loudly.

"Your bid, Omar," replied his wife. "Don't point."

"Oh, er, pass," he said vaguely.

She glared at him, and craned around toward Miss Nadi. I sat nearby on a low couch where I could watch the legendary beauty unobserved. Her almost Egyptian profile, her long, bejeweled fingers, her vivid coloring, made me feel small and washed out.

She had been speaking to a tall, broad-shouldered, sandy-haired man in a gray lounge suit. He had a typically American way of speaking—a kind of breezy exaggeration—which softened the most outrageous remarks with a kind of good humor. And he had a very nice voice, warm and rich. "Have a heart, Miss Nadi," he said. "My editor will boil me in oil if he finds out I've sailed with you and didn't get an exclusive story. Without your help, I'll just have to piece together a story from what I can glean elsewhere, and it'll be harder on you."

She narrowed her eyes. No editor in the world, I felt sure, could be more threatening than Vera Nadi as she looked at that moment—like a cat, ready to pounce.

"It was magnificent, that look," I said to Aunt Hermione later as we prepared for bed. "I'd give anything to be able to summon up a look like that."

"Oh, Iris, you don't mean that," said my aunt. "It's so cheap and theatrical, that sort of thing. The woman is undoubtedly nothing but a common adventuress."

"If she's an adventuress, she isn't a common one," I replied.

And we slept, unaware that with each revolution of the *Irenia*'s screws, we were being brought closer to very real adventure, adventure I would never forget.

CHAPTER TWO

I was surprised to see such a good turnout among our tablemates at breakfast. Aunt Hermione had remained in bed, murmuring about the possibility of some biscuits and milk, but only after she was certain she was able to handle them. The *Irenia* had hit a North Atlantic squall, and her heavy, steady roll had been complicated by a wicked, unpredictable pitch.

Judge Omar Griffin, true to his word, had rearranged the seatings, and he and his wife now sat at our table. The judge was a tall, lanky man with a shiny, bald head. His dark, rather ferocious eyebrows slid around his forehead when he talked. His face could have been made of rubber; it twitched and grimaced with each sentence.

He was giving the people at our table the itinerary of his recent European tour in a deep, golden voice. ". . . and then we went to Rome. Didn't care much for it myself. You've seen one broken hunk of marble, you've seen 'em all. And I couldn't understand a word, in spite of my Latin. Louise liked it, though. She's crazy about those old Romans and Greeks."

Louise was a quiet woman with pinched little features, probably the result of years of listening. Her hair was arranged elaborately in gray loops, and she had shrewd gray-blue eyes.

"But we got ourselves a guide. Bright young fellow. Spoke pretty good English," the judge rattled on, oblivious to the slightly green cast of his tablemates. Only the colonel looked fit.

I watched him go lustily at his kippers and eggs. It made me a little queasy. I never eat much breakfast. Perhaps it's because at home I saw to it that everyone else got theirs. I looked dubiously at a piece of toast and sipped coffee tentatively.

Colonel Marris looked up at me, wiping grease from his moustache with a large napkin. "Not eating, Miss Cooper? Bit off your feed, eh? Not a touch of the old mal de mer, I hope." He slid another egg onto his plate.

Norman Twist looked up from his similarly hearty breakfast. "Oh, goodness, I hope not!"

"I am an excellent sailor," I replied firmly.

Colonel Marris slit open his egg yolk and began to sponge it up with bits of toast. "All in the mind. Simply a matter of setting your mind to it. Don't give in. Never been seasick in my life. Haven't allowed myself to be."

The judge, speaking to no one in particular, continued the story of his tour. "These Balkan countries, now, never could figure where the hell we were. I learned the capitals of everything when I was a schoolboy, but the war changed it all around. Say, professor, are you from that part of the world?"

The professor didn't answer. He stared across the room. We all looked in the direction of his stare and saw Vera Nadi, breakfasting alone. It was strange to see her in the morning. She looked like some waxy, night-blooming flower.

"Vera Nadi," said the judge appreciatively, "in person."

The professor, looking a trifle embarrassed, went for the coffeepot with a trembling hand. I looked closely at him and detected a hint of a blush beneath the green. "Extraordinary-looking woman. You know her, judge?" His tone was casual, but he seemed remarkably interested. I wondered if I would ever invoke so much male fascination.

"*Everyone* knows Vera Nadi," exclaimed the judge, shocked at the other man's ignorance. "The moving picture star. She was *A Woman's Revenge* and *Moroccan Dream.*

And something about twins separated at birth. Let's see, what was it called? *Coronation of a Gypsy*."

Mrs. Griffin rolled her eyes expressively and retrieved a collection of cutlery as it slid across the tablecloth. "Omar just loves the movies," she said. "And he reads all those awful little gossip sheets."

"Sure do," he replied. "Darned interesting. Say, you know who's sailing with us? I read all about it in London. What's the name of that paper?"

"*The Tattler*, perhaps?" said Mr. Twist.

"Yup. That's it. Anyway, the Comte de Lanier is on this ship. He's going to marry one of these madcap debutantes, Marjorie Klepp, heiress to the cotter-pin fortune. There's the count over there." He pointed across the salon to a slim, dark man.

"Don't point, Omar," said Mrs. Griffin.

"Mrs. Griffin thinks I'm just an old back-fence gossip," chortled the judge. "But it's human nature I'm interested in, human nature. Comes naturally in my profession. I see all kinds in front of the bench."

Mrs. Griffin turned to me in a confidential manner. "I always say men are worse gossips than women," she said.

I did feel rather green around the gills but I hadn't mentioned it at the table. I knew the colonel would have gone on about mind over matter, and although I subscribed to the same theory, I didn't want to hear it from anyone else. And Mr. Twist had looked at me with such concern, and I didn't want him to feel sorry for me. He was the kind of young man you feel you must be kind to, and the kind who then interprets this charitable impulse as romantic interest. I resolved to be polite but distant with him.

I am not really seasick, I said to myself, attributing my unsteadiness to the kippery atmosphere in the dining salon, and all those greasy fried eggs staring up at me.

A brisk walk around the deck was just what I needed, I

thought. And not the sheltered boat deck, but the promenade deck, where fresh air would engulf me.

The promenade deck was almost abandoned. It was rough, and probably getting rougher. The deck was wet with heavy spray, the lifeboats creaked and groaned in their davits, and I set as direct a course as I could against the roll and pitch of the ship.

The ship's doctor stood by the rail. He looked miserable. How unfortunate, I thought, that a ship's doctor should suffer from seasickness. But then I noticed his face didn't bear the haggard, pale expression of the seasick, but rather a puffy, ruddy look. I remembered hearing about ship's doctors not always being suited to private practice, and I wondered if the poor man drank and was seeking the spray and the salt as a remedy for the symptoms of the morning after. I resolved to stay well on the voyage, and pressed on.

I met Colonel Marris, walking the other way around, gulping large amounts of sea air, and I smiled brightly, trying to look hale and hearty.

The sea was rough, steel gray with plenty of white, and the sky was gray, too. But despite the roughness and the chill, I was beginning to feel better. I could even look at the tilt of the rail angled against the sky without too much dizziness, and I began to develop a gait that worked with the sea instead of against it.

Behind me I heard the cries of children. Against the gust of the wind, they seemed very far away, but they were soon abreast of me, running and jumping, oblivious to the harshness. There were two of them, a boy and a girl, both blond, bundled in identical dark coats. The boy swooped in the air with a toy airplane, and the girl, the smaller of the two, shrieked with delight.

I was very fond of children. I had raised my brothers and sisters, with some help from Aunt Hermione, after my mother died. I enjoyed watching these two and was glad when they approached.

"My airplane is a Fokker," said the boy importantly.

"How nice," I replied.

"My daddy's been in a real airplane. Have you?"

"No. But I'd like to."

"If I went in a real plane, I'd like to go in a Fokker," the boy said.

The little girl watched me silently, a smudgy finger in her mouth, while her brother talked. Presently a tall woman joined us, and herded the children toward her. "I hope they aren't bothering you," she said in clipped tones.

"Not at all. I'm fond of children."

The woman bent over her charges, tying a shoe, buttoning a coat, scrubbing the girl's face with a handkerchief. "These are very energetic children," she said meaningfully.

She spoke to them softly in German, and they scampered ahead. She followed closely. I watched her tall, narrow form. Her carriage was almost a military carriage. She could have been what my father called "a handsome woman" if she weren't so obviously—in her plain clothes and sensible shoes, with an unattractive hat pulled down over her hair—a governess. I felt a stab of sadness for her, and then I felt an odd little thrill as I spied the piano player standing by the rail, looking out to sea. His warning had unnerved me, but I had decided that it was some sort of foolishness meant to be exciting and seductive. It had made a strong impression on me, but now, by the light of day, it all seemed slightly silly.

"How do you do?" he asked.

"I'm just fine," I answered. "Do you have any more obscure warnings for me this morning?" I added cheerfully. "Somehow I have never felt less as if there were danger afoot."

"You are wrong to laugh at me," he said. "I meant what I said. But never mind. Perhaps you will remain untouched. You have sort of a halo about you; it must be that cloud of red-gold hair. You look protected. Perhaps you were born under a lucky star."

"You look as if you had been born under a dark star," I said. And he did. Without the dark, saturnine cast to his features, he would have been too handsome.

"I suppose I have." He scowled.

The professor plodded past, still looking pale. We nodded.

"I hate that man," said the pianist casually, after he had passed. "And I don't care who knows it."

"Professor Probrislow? Why do you hate him? Nobody is really worth hating, are they? Hate is bad for your disposition."

"What do you know of hate?" he sneered. "Or of love? Or of anything?"

I decided I hated *him*. "Well, if you have any more peculiar warnings, attach them to my cabin door with a dagger. Just sign them, 'A Friend.' And be sure to misspell 'friend.' The *i* and *e* are always reversed in peculiar warnings," I snapped.

I was still puzzling over this strange exchange when I passed Mr. Twist, sitting in a deck chair, well-muffled by a lap robe. He grinned at me amiably from beneath a tweed cap and began to rise, balancing a cup of some steaming liquid.

"No, no. Don't get up. You'll get untucked," I said.

He indicated the deck chair next to him and opened his mouth, but I murmured something about my obligatory morning lap of the deck, and pressed on. How I wish I hadn't done that. Had I but known—well, I couldn't really have known, I suppose. Mr. Twist was simply the sort of person who inspired you to keep walking. Anyway, now cured of my queasiness, I decided to explore the *Irenia*, and discovered the ship's library. There I met the ship's conductress, a partridge-like Scotswoman with a crisp head of auburn hair. She suggested some Ethel M. Dell novels, but I chose instead

some thrillers with soupy covers and a travel book. I took
another half turn of the promenade deck, observing a
snoozing Mr. Twist, and Vera Nadi, clutching the rail and
looking out onto the wild sea. She smiled a scarlet smile, and
the wind whipped her dark hair out behind her. She looked
half crazed. It wasn't normal to smile out at a storm like
that. I shuddered.

I found Aunt Hermione in the lounge, drinking coffee. "I
really feel so much better, Iris dear. You do *shame* me into
it. And, of course, how can one sleep in one's cabin when you
hearty types are tramping on the deck over one's head? Iris,
I've just met the captain. Such a nice man. *Very* reassuring
about icebergs. It must be a lonely life, a life at sea." She
sighed romantically.

"I saw the doctor on deck," I said. "And you know, he
didn't look well at all." I flung myself into a wicker chair at
her side.

"Probably drinks like a fish," said Aunt Hermione
placidly. "I can't think why they all do. I mean, we've been
on three or four steamers on this trip, and half of them, the
ship's doctors I mean, *drank*. Of course, on that trip through
the China Sea I can understand. I mean, all those *mission-
aries* on board were quite enough to try anyone's Christian
fortitude."

We talked of our travels and drank coffee and ate biscuits.

"You know, Iris," said Aunt Hermione after a time, "I
hope you realize what a wonderful job you've done with the
children. After we all lost poor Julia, well, it was wonderful
the way you took charge. But I don't want you to worry
about them too much while you're away at school. I'll look in
on them often, you know."

I smiled. "They'll be fine," I said. How wonderful it would
be, I thought, to be free of responsibility. To be able to know
that I could close my door and be free of constant in-
terruptions. To not have to worry about chills and fevers, or

mediate squabbles. I had done it all cheerfully. But I had learned, too, how much I needed time for myself.

Aunt Hermione had understood. She had insisted that I go away to college. Father had resisted when she brought it up, but she had won. And she had taken me all around the world and bought lovely clothes for me, and had even had my hair bobbed for me in Paris. And about time, too, I thought. The barber had asked if I wanted the thick red-gold braid he'd chopped off, but I had just smiled and told him no.

My hair felt very free and breezy and looked so much better with the new hats. Best of all, my face sort of came into its own. I decided it was a very nice face indeed, framed by some curls, instead of dragged down by all that hair. I wondered if they'd disapprove of my hair and clothes back home in Portland. I hoped they would, just a little.

I sat, thinking happy thoughts of the independence I'd be enjoying at Stanford in September, just a month away, and looking at Aunt Hermione's kind face and drinking coffee, when the door of the lounge swung open and a deck steward ran through the smoking room calling for the doctor.

The doctor emerged, pulling on his coat, and sent for his medical kit while startled passengers set up agitated murmurs.

I suppose everyone acts differently in emergencies. I sprang after the doctor, and so did Colonel Marris. The steward led us to a deck chair, and the huddled form of Norman Twist.

"He won't wake," said the steward. "I think he's . . ."

"Dead," said the doctor, and bent over Mr. Twist, feeling for his heart.

"Hullo," said the colonel, and inched the deck chair forward. Between the wooden slats of the chair, and going straight into Norman Twist's back, was a knife. A ship's paper knife, actually, bearing the words "S.S. *Irenia*, Blue Star Line" on the solid brass handle.

There was a nasty, dark patch around the hilt of the knife. The body fell forward, a strange mass of crumpled tweed. The doctor pulled the lap robe over Mr. Twist's head. "Fetch another steward, and get this body to my surgery," he said quietly to the man who'd sounded the alarm.

More passengers came forward and stood around in a hushed circle. The cardinal murmured some words in Latin and reached out to touch the body. Louise Griffin narrowed her gray-blue eyes and said in an angry whisper, "I don't think the boy was a Roman Catholic." The cardinal nodded gravely and looked confused at the same time.

We stood there for some time. It was as if we weren't sure of the correct behavior for the situation, so we remained quiet and solemn. The throb of the engines and the chilly salt in the air and the glossy, wet expanse of deck tilting to and fro seemed all the more vivid in the quiet. Next to me, the colonel muttered, "Shouldn't have happened." I saw the glint of tears in his rather bulging blue eyes, and instinctively put a hand on his arm. He looked at me, startled, and I withdrew it, thinking he though the gesture too familiar, although perhaps he was simply startled to find himself crying.

After what seemed like an interminable length of time, the two stewards came. They stood awkwardly around the body, not quite sure how to go about carrying it, and they were too embarrassed to discuss the logistics of transporting it out loud. Finally the first steward began to lift the body by its arms, and the other, responding to this silent cue, seized the ankles. I noted with a feeling akin to horror that Mr. Twist wore a pair of flamboyant socks, apple green with extravagant purple clocks, and that his shoes were almost mustard-colored. Although they were well-polished, they were definitely down to the heel.

Finally the doctor suggested that the stewards carry the chair with the body in it, rather than wrestle the body free.

They looked relieved. "And for God's sake, stay out of the public rooms on the way to my surgery," said the doctor. "Here. Better follow me." He took off down the deck. They make a grotesque procession, the doctor with his bag and the stewards struggling under the burden of the deck chair with its slain occupant.

CHAPTER THREE

Now that it was over, and Mr. Twist's body was out of sight, I began to tremble. Colonel Marris put a large hand around my shoulder. "Spot of brandy is what you'll be needing," he said gently.

Slightly dazed, I followed him to the smoking room bar. Warm, dim, and nearly empty, it looked rather as I imagined gentlemen's clubs looked. There was a vast, murky Oriental carpet, clusters of ugly squat palms in brass tubs, and groups of blue leather chairs arranged around low dark tables trimmed with brass rails. An ornately carved mahogany bar, backed by a mirror, ran across the length of the room. There was a faint scent of stale cigar in the air.

We sat and watched a steward remove a framed notice admonishing the passengers to be vigilant about card sharps. He replaced it with another that read: "Professional Card Sharps Are Sailing Aboard This Vessel. Passengers Are Advised to Refrain from Playing Cards with Those Unknown to Them." He gave the glass on the notice a few neat wipes with a white cloth, and Colonel Marris ordered two brandies.

We were silent until the glasses filled to the brim with the amber fluid arrived. I swallowed, and felt the blood in my temples dance.

"Mr. Twist," I began slowly, "hardly is the type, or *was* the type, I suppose I should say, to get himself—"

"Stabbed in the back," said the colonel with a firmness that startled me. I was relieved that my companion wasn't mealymouthed about death. It was such a bother framing

31

euphemisms about "the departed," as I usually had to do when discussing dead people.

"Exactly. Stabbed in the back," I said.

"Most peculiar," was the reply. "Pleasant young ass. Can't imagine what he'd do to invoke a murderer's wrath."

I gulped. "I saw him sitting there all morning. I thought he was asleep." I felt suddenly that I should have stopped and stayed with Mr. Twist, and not walked on as I had done.

"Did he say anything to you?" asked the colonel. "Anything about being in danger?"

"Goodness no," I replied. I thought of the piano player's warning, but I rattled on: "Mr. Twist seemed so ordinary." Why didn't I mention the piano player's warning to Colonel Marris? On some impulse I didn't stop to analyze, I thrust the strange comments to the back of my mind. "Rather bashful and simple and ordinary."

The colonel's ruddy face had paled, and I noticed a new intensity in the protruding blue eyes. "I've led a full life, Miss Cooper," he said softly. "Seen action in the trenches, been in various kinds of out-of-the-way spots where this sort of bushwhacking goes on as a matter of course. But there's nothing so terrifying as to see cold-blooded murder in a civilized setting. I don't mind saying that an outrage of this type gives a chap quite a turn."

"What will they do now?" I queried.

"Hmm. Oh. The captain's probably wiring the company. Out here in the mid-Atlantic, who knows? May be detained in Montreal."

"The killer is still on board," I said stupidly. It had just dawned on me. "I mean he must be."

"That's right. And a very daring killer, too."

"Do you think some kind of maniac did it?" I asked.

"Seems to me a maniac would brandish an ax and carry on," he replied gravely. "This business is too calculated to suit me."

• • •

"Iris dear," said Aunt Hermione as she dug into her handbag. "We *must* go to our cabin and lie down. I'm so upset. That poor young man. Of course, we barely knew him, but he was young, and rather helpless. I *know* I had my smelling salts here."

She was animated enough without them. "I'm sure you'll be fine," I said in my calmest tones. "Shall we send for a sherry?"

"Yes, dear. What a good idea. And maybe some sandwiches later."

We made our way through the lounge and walked past the wireless office where the sandy-haired reporter stood grimacing. "The captain says he won't let me wire my paper," he complained. "I don't know what my editor will say. This is a swell story. What did you know about this Twist fellow, anything? You sat at his table, right? Say, what was the murdered man's last meal?"

"Why, the poor boy's not cold in his grave yet," said Aunt Hermione.

"My aunt is upset," I said.

"Of course," he said soothingly. "It is a shock."

She glared at him, and I hurried her along.

"I wonder if the poor boy had any people," she said, browsing among the bon voyage baskets in our cabin, and selecting a pear to accompany her sherry. "I suppose the captain will find out. Really, he didn't seem unbalanced or anything, but do you suppose he took his own life?"

"Suicides, as they say in all the books, never stab themselves in the back," I replied.

"I suppose not. Iris dear, whatever made you rush out there like that?"

"I don't know. It seemed the right thing to do at the time."

"Well, you certainly are a *brave* girl. I remember when your brother Freddie broke his leg and you held it all together until the doctor came, even though it flopped around *most* unnaturally. Was it gruesome? Mr. Twist, I mean, not poor Freddie's leg."

"No." I sighed. "He was pale and crumpled, sort of like a bundle of clothes. There wasn't much blood."

"Well, that's nice." She seemed quite cheery again. "I suppose dinner will be awkward. Poor Professor Probrislow must be quite shaken. Although perhaps if I suggest bridge, it will take his mind off all this unpleasantness. You know, Iris, I think black would be excessive. We really didn't know him at all well. Maybe just something suitably drab. Perhaps my pearl gray moiré silk?"

At dinner, Professor Probrislow seemed quite composed, and showed no reticence in discussing his slain secretary.

"So young, so tragic. Could I trouble you for the asparagus? Ah, thank you. And the sauce . . . not really enough lemon, is there? I can't imagine what fiend has perpetrated such an unspeakable offense." I imagined he was referring to the murder and not to the hollandaise.

"How well did you know the boy, professor?" asked the judge.

"Not well at all. I had only recently engaged him."

"What was he supposed to do for you?"

"Oh, keep track of my appointments and so forth. These lecture tours are quite harrowing." He gestured vaguely.

"Did the poor boy have any family?" asked Aunt Hermione.

"He never mentioned any."

"He told me his family was all gone," I said.

"Yes. There. You see, he had no family." Professor Probrislow eyed the potatoes near me. I anticipated his request and passed them his way.

"What I want to know," said Louise Griffin, "is who killed him, and are we in danger?"

We were silent for a moment as the professor helped himself to potatoes, grating the spoon unpleasantly along the porcelain.

"Mrs. Griffin has a point," said the colonel. "We must do what we can to apprehend the criminal. Can't have people being stabbed to death on a British passenger ship. Good Lord, it's an outrage."

"The captain," began the professor carefully, "has asked several of us with an expert knowledge of crime to make preliminary inquiries. The judge and I will assist him in these investigations."

"I see," said the colonel. He sounded hurt, as if he felt left out. It must be hard, I thought, for a retired military man to be excluded from running things. "Did a little intelligence work in my time," he said gruffly. "Had a knack for the work. Perhaps I could be of some assistance."

The professor shrugged.

"Good idea," said the judge kindly. "My experience is pretty limited. We get pretty straightforward mayhem in our neck of the woods. In Lewiston, people shoot each other."

"Except the foreman up at the mill. He took a ballpeen hammer to Mabel Carruthers," added Mrs. Griffin. She put a hand to her elaborate loopy coiffure, as if to feel whether everything was in place. Everything was.

"I'll mention it to the captain, Marris," said the judge affably.

"Glad to be of help," said the colonel gratefully.

"Professor, you must have some idea what kind of criminal is responsible," said Aunt Hermione.

"Yes," said the judge. "Does the method strike you as characteristic of a certain type?"

"Stabbings in the back are very ordinary, I fear." The professor polished his pince-nez with his napkin. "Interesting rash of this sort of thing in Vienna in the eighties. Often impulsive."

"Well, this couldn't have been impulsive," said the colonel. "Looked pretty calculated to me."

"The criminal mind is a complex labyrinth of strange, hidden impulses," began the professor. I imagined he was giving us a part of his lecture. "The darkest side of the human soul remains a mystery, even to those of us who have devoted our lives to the science of the mind. We are only beginning to add to the work of the pioneers in the field of criminal behavior. Cesare Lombroso, for instance, who—"

"Lot of rubbish," snorted the colonel. "Measuring thumbs and earlobes. Sheer nonsense."

"I see you are familiar with my field," said the professor coldly.

"Read a bit. Damned interesting. But I've seen things in my time, can't be explained by scientific mumbo-jumbo. Young officer in Poonah, for instance. Nice young lad. An Englishman of the better type. No stubby thumbs or beady eyes. Handsome lad, well-brought-up, good family. Strangled the major's wife in broad daylight. Crime of passion. Some sordid business going on between them. These outposts can get sticky."

"I bet they can," said the judge cheerfully.

I looked at Norman Twist's empty chair, and Mrs. Griffin's question haunted me. "Are we in danger?" she had asked placidly. I wanted to know the answer, and deep inside me, the question gave me a strange thrill.

The next day at lunch I found a note on my plate. It asked me to come meet with the committee the professor had told us about. Apparently, only those who had been on the promenade deck when Mr. Twist sat in his deck chair would be questioned.

"With a hundred or more passengers," explained the judge, "we've decided to talk only to the ones who were on deck. The deck steward kept pretty good track of who was there. Not too many of 'em, either, thank goodness. The weather was lousy, and most people were only up to the boat deck, if they were on deck at all. We'll take their passports and note down anything pertinent and submit a full report to the authorities in Canada. Seems the best we can do."

Aunt Hermione was thrilled I had been asked to appear. "Remember everything they ask you, and tell me all about it, Iris," she said.

I promised I would, and then added teasingly, "You know, of course, Aunt Hermione, this means I'm a suspect."

"Nonsense," she replied. "How *dare* they suggest such a thing? I shall speak to the captain."

I dissuaded her from this course of action.

I looked forward to the questioning. I wanted desperately to be of whatever help I could in bringing the killer to justice. It seemed intensely important that Mr. Twist's death not go unavenged.

I reported to the captain's cabin and tried to look blasé about being a witness in a murder inquiry. I sat in a straight-backed chair in a tiny vestibule and watched the purser check my name off a list.

The young American reporter came into the waiting area, smiled a wide, rather gleaming smile, and sat down beside me. I turned my head a little away from him, deciding that I didn't like his manner. There was something just a little too familiar about it.

"I bet you saw something, something that will lead to the solution of the mystery," he said eagerly.

I told him I had not.

"Well, maybe you could make up something for my paper. Save me the trouble."

Shocked, I turned to face him. He had a rather sportily handsome face, with a kind of openness about it that was strangely at odds with his shrewd, gray-green eyes.

"Just kidding, just kidding." He laughed, obviously

amused at the disapproval in my expression. "I don't make up stuff. I get the truth. The real goods."

A little, bespectacled man with a cherubic face burst into the small room and flung himself on the purser. I remembered seeing him fluttering through the lounge and chatting about the ship's concert. I'd pegged him as the ship bore, a type that never varied from vessel to vessel, and one who applied boundless energy to the task of organizing strained and contrived merriment among the passengers.

"I must see the captain," he wailed in a reedy midwestern voice. "I need to know whether or not to proceed with the ship's concert. Some of the passengers have suggested that considering the, er, unfortunate circumstances, such levity would be in less than good taste. I, however, feel a jolly evening such as the one I'm planning will cheer us all up. I'm sure the captain will agree. And when I tell the nay-sayers that I have his support, we can go on with the plans."

The man, whose name was Mr. Ogle, paused for breath and launched forth once more: "It should be a real corker of a concert. Miss Nadi has consented to give a dramatic reading from *Salomé*, although I've persuaded her to keep the racier bits out, and I brought my cello along just for the occasion. How can anyone protest, when it all goes in aid of seamen's charities?"

"You'll have to wait until the captain conducts this, er, other business," said the purser.

"I must see him *now*." Mr. Ogle's voice had climbed an octave with agitation. "The gunnysack races are about to begin."

"Gosh," said the reporter at my side. "Gunnysack races, ship's concert. Don't you ever rest, Mr. Ogle?"

Mr. Ogle looked at him distractedly. "Hmm? Oh, it's Mr. Clancy. Glad I ran into you. You've won the mileage pool. The smoking room steward has your winnings. And I meant to ask you for some help with the ship's concert. Being a

literary man, perhaps you'd be good enough to help us with
the program. We'd like something special. Perhaps some
rhymed couplets. What do you say?"

"I write for money," said Mr. Clancy shamelessly. He
stretched out his long legs and hooked his arms around the
back of his chair.

Mr. Ogle frowned. "This is supposed to be *fun*, Mr. Clancy.
Besides, the whole thing's in aid of seamen's charities.
Widows and orphans of drowned sailors, that sort of thing."

"Sure, sure, okay," said Mr. Clancy. "Can't let down the
widows and orphans."

Mr. Ogle favored him with a wide smile. "Wonderful, Mr.
Clancy, I knew I could count on you." He turned to the
purser once again. "I'll just take a minute of the captain's
time. He knows me well. I've sailed with this line every year
for twenty years. I've become a regular fixture."

"Yes indeed, Mr. Ogle," replied the purser. "You certainly
have."

"I hold the endurance record for deck laps on the Blue
Star Line," Mr. Ogle said to me over his shoulder as the
exasperated purser ushered him into the captain's cabin.
"Thirty-two laps in one day."

He flitted through the door and emerged a few minutes
later, a look of triumph in his face. "I knew he wouldn't say
no to widows and orphans," he said happily. "Mr. Clancy, I'll
have all the information for the program sent to your cabin.
I've lined up some wonderful talent. It'll be a rousing show."

"As long as you don't have a whistling solo or a Swede
comedian," muttered the reporter.

"We *do* have a whistling solo," said Mr. Ogle, his eyebrows
forming two dramatic points. "Mrs. Ogle always does her
whistling solo at ship's concerts. It's a perennial favorite."

"See here, Mr. Ogle. I really didn't know." Mr. Clancy surprised me by blushing.

"I really didn't know," he said to me helplessly, after a

rather put-out Mr. Ogle had left. He turned to the purser. "Ever caught Mrs. Ogle's act?"

"Many times," said the purser. " 'Stout-Hearted Men' is the selection she favors." Mr. Clancy burst into deep laughter, and I repressed a giggle myself. Then the door to the inner sanctum opened, and someone within spoke to the purser. "Send in Miss Cooper, will you?"

CHAPTER FOUR

*T*he four members of the committee rose as I entered, and I sat down amid the chorus of their scraping wooden chairs. There was an odd symmetry to the men; two were balding and clean-shaven, two wore beards. The captain's beard was a magnificent dark spade shape, shot through with silver. The professor ran a hand through his soft pale brown beard, and I noticed how long his fingers were. They all sat at a long oak table, and the colonel shuffled papers before him in an official-looking manner. I imagined he was terribly pleased to be on the committee, and his manner indicated that he felt comfortable acting in an official capacity. The judge seemed to be presiding over the inquiry. He looked very solemn, unlike his usual gregarious self, and addressed me in his deep, golden tones.

"You understand, Miss Cooper, what we are doing here. This is a preliminary inquiry to assist the proper authorities when they take up the case."

I nodded.

"Now, you are Iris Cooper. How old are you?"

"Nineteen. I'll be twenty next month."

"And where do you live?"

"Portland, Oregon."

"And you are returning home?"

"Yes, my aunt and I have just finished traveling around the world."

"Was Mr. Twist known to you before you boarded this vessel?"

"No. I met him here, at our table."

41

"Did you speak to Mr. Twist?"

"Just a little."

"And what did he say?"

"Anything could be important," interjected the colonel. "Twist seems to have been somewhat of a mystery man."

"Well, on deck, we just said hello. But the evening before, he told me he'd been a librarian. He was very anxious to see America. He came from a little village where he was badly behaved as a child, and his family were all gone."

"Did you form any impression of him?" asked the judge.

"He seemed very ordinary. Almost too ordinary. And rather shy but eager, if you know what I mean."

"Did you notice anything unusual about him on deck, the day he died?"

"No. He just sat in his deck chair, with a cup of tea or something. I passed him once, and we nodded and then I passed him again when I did another half lap. He seemed to be asleep." It occurred to me he may have been dead then, and I shuddered.

"Who else did you see on deck?"

"I remember Colonel Marris, the cardinal, those blond children and their governess . . ."

The captain was writing furiously.

"Am I going too fast? Maybe I can help you. I take shorthand. To help my father in his business." I tried to look calm, but my heart was racing at the thought that I could join the group.

"Well, gentlemen?" said the judge. "Should we take the young lady on as a court reporter?" Judge Griffin seemed very amiable about enlarging the committee.

The professor looked dubious.

"Splendid idea," said the colonel. I hardly thought his opinion counted for much; after all, he'd weaseled his way onto the committee himself, but the captain surprised me by agreeing.

"Why not? It'll make our job much easier."

"This inquiry must be discreet," said the professor.

"Oh, come on, Probrislow," said Judge Griffin. "If she's the killer, we can keep a better eye on her here." He laughed heartily.

I was insulted at being thought incapable of murder, but delighted at the opportunity to follow the case more closely.

"Very well." The professor smiled thinly at me.

"Now, we'll get you started as soon as we finish with your own testimony here. Who else did you see on the promenade deck?"

"The doctor. He looked unwell." The captain coughed delicately. "And the professor here, and the piano player."

"The one who danced with you," said the judge.

"Fraternizing with the passengers, was he?" The captain frowned.

When the questioning was completed, he asked for my passport, and I handed it over. It was probably a device intended to make sure no witnesses vanished before the Canadian authorities had a chance to question them. We waited for the next passenger while I arranged my notebook.

The arrival of Vera Nadi caused a flutter of masculine approval among the committee members. Preceded into the captain's cabin by a cloud of strong, sultry perfume, she sat forward in her chair and arranged her furs carefully over her shoulders.

She had, it appeared, taken a turn on deck because "I love the sea at its wildest. I feel very close to the sea, and love to observe it in all its moods. Like me, it is ever changing; sometimes calm, sometimes wild and wind-lashed."

"Yes, yes," said the colonel. "Did you see this Twist fellow on deck?"

"Twist. You mean the man who died. No. I did not."

"Whom did you see?"

"His eminence, the cardinal. The Comte de Lanier—an old

friend of mine, by the way—and, let me see, that is all. Perhaps I saw some children. Yes, some children, but I do not
know how many. More than one."

"Thank you, Miss Nadi," said the judge. "We appreciate
your assisting us."

"There is something else you should perhaps know," she
said. "Did you know there was a blackmailer on board?" She
smiled and leaned back in her chair to gauge the effect of her
revelation.

The effect was spectacular. I glanced around the table,
and everyone was evidently stunned. After a suitable pause,
Miss Nadi continued. "Yes," she said, placing the back of her
gloved hand on her forehead, "a horrible, nasty little note,
demanding money for silence."

Judge Griffin seemed flustered. "Naturally, madame,
being in the public eye, you are no doubt a likely target for
this sort of thing."

Vera Nadi smiled again. "The price one pays for fame. I
am accustomed to such outrages. There are many, many
lunatics who weave me into their fantasies. And the ordinary
fans are a trial, too. Sad little people, eager to hear every
detail of my life. How paltry their own poor lives must be.
They read all about me in those hideous little magazines."

The judge had the grace to blush.

"Well, who," asked the colonel, "sent the note?"

"I don't know. It was signed 'One Who Knows Your
Secret.' " Vera Nadi rattled a diamond bracelet.

" 'One Who Knows Your Secret,' " repeated the judge with
relish. "My, my."

"Well, if you didn't know who the blackmailer was," said
the colonel with a trace of impatience, "How were you to
pay him?"

Vera Nadi shrugged. "He said he would find me."

"And did he?"

"Not yet."

"You said, 'he,' just now," continued Colonel Marris, with a thoughtful tug at his moustache. "Do you have reason to believe the blackmailer was a man?"

"Not really. 'I'll find you' is what the note said, precisely."

"Have you still got the note?"

"I destroyed it. It was so distasteful. . . ."

"You didn't respond to it in any fashion?" he continued.

"I thought it inadvisable. In any case, I am ashamed of nothing I have done." She paused. "Everything I have done has been for love."

The judge beamed at her. "Gallant, madame. Gallant. Much like the heroine of *A Woman's Revenge*."

"Ah, you know my work." She smiled.

"Then you will have no objection to our knowing the contents of the note," said the colonel.

The professor spoke up for the first time. "Surely this is not necessary. This lady has been forthright with us. It would be impertinent to pursue this."

"Not at all," said Miss Nadi eagerly. "The note threatened to reveal to the world a passion, yes, a requited passion, which I once shared with a certain noble personage. It was a brief but idyllic interlude in my life. I loved him and have no regrets. It was many years ago, when I was very, very young." She seemed to gaze beyond us all. The judge sighed.

"Do you think," said the colonel, "that young Twist was blackmailing you?"

"Possibly. I had imagined someone else to be the blackmailer."

"Who?" inquired the captain.

"That horrid reporter. With the square jaw. A despicable man."

"And have you any reasons for your suspicions?" asked the colonel.

"He made a nuisance of himself. He threatened to write lies about me if I did not grant him an interview."

"I see," said the colonel. "Well, please let us know if you have any further communication from this person. Although with all this fuss about a murder he may lie low."

"If he's still alive," said the professor. "It seems pretty likely to me that our victim was a blackmailer, and someone"—he eyed Vera Nadi significantly—"who objected to being blackmailed, killed him."

"There'll be time for theories later," said the judge sternly. "Right now we're simply collecting facts." He turned back to Miss Nadi. "Is there anything else you wish to tell us?"

"No," she said thoughtfully, gazing at the professor as he fitted a cigarette into an amber holder. "But if something comes to mind, perhaps..."

"Thank you so much," gushed the judge. "And your secret is safe with us," he added.

I thought that hardly likely; I imagined Vera Nadi's royal escapade would make the rounds of Lewiston, Idaho, very quickly.

"Something about that story strikes a familiar note," mused the colonel, after Miss Nadi had gone, leaving her passport behind. "That story you told the other night, Griffin, something about a milliner's assistant?"

"Say!" The judge lit up. "Could that be Miss Nadi?"

"How did the yarn go again?" asked the colonel. "It was late, and I, well..."

The judge settled back to tell the story that had so obviously bored the colonel before. "One of our guides in the Balkans, he told us about this king, some king they had there before the war. Ran off with some little gal—she was a milliner's assistant, brought hats up to the palace for the ladies to try on, and she caught the king's eye. Yessir, he fell pretty hard. Ran off with her to the French Riviera. There was quite a flap. Contributed to the downfall of the royal house. Seems the king took some important stuff with him when he flew the coop, state secrets or something, and stuff that proves you're really the king, like the royal seal or something. Anyway, and here's the interesting part, the little milliner's assistant went on to become a famous motion picture star. The guide fellow had seen her in American pictures. Of course, they get Hollywood pictures ten years late over there. But he recognized her. The name didn't ring a bell though, and I know all the stars."

"What was her name?" inquired the colonel. "And who was the king?"

"I never forget a name," said the judge. "Rosa Nadescu. Probably some extra girl. But I forget the king. These Balkan places, never could figure it out. This girl was supposed to be really something. Barely twenty, but she knew her way around, I guess. They managed to drag the king back, but I guess it was never the same afterward. He put a bullet through his head, and they got a new guy, but then the war wiped out the whole place."

"Vera Nadi is no doubt a stage name," said the colonel. "Perhaps it's never been legally changed." The judge flipped through Vera Nadi's American passport. "Great suffering catfish, here it is! Rosa Nadescu. Well, what do you know!"

"And the king," said the colonel, "may well have been King Nicholas of Graznia. A most irresponsible monarch. Mind you, some of our English kings have sowed their oats, but, but God, they stick by the job. You'll never see an English king give up the throne for a woman he loves."

"Hmm," said the judge, still studying Miss Nadi's passport. "It says here she's Romanian-born. That's funny. I distinctly remember reading in *Movie Mirages* that Vera Nadi was born in a harem in Constantinople.

"Anyway," he continued, "this story I got in the Balkans is straight. Our guide had been a footman at the palace, and he got the real lowdown."

"Our blackmailer, Twist or whoever else, could have got

the story right here on board. There were several of us in the bar when you told it. Anyone could have heard it," said the colonel.

The judge indeed had a powerful voice. It was easy to imagine his election orations.

"Can we proceed with the next passenger?" interrupted the captain. "I'd like to finish as quickly as possible."

"Yes," said the professor, eyeing me, "let's discuss the details later. We must be discreet."

The next witness was the steward, a slight man with thinning hair, who had brought Mr. Twist a cup of Bovril at nine-thirty. Mr. Twist had not given him a tip, in spite of the fact that hot drinks were served to everybody at ten-thirty, and Twist's Bovril had had to be specially ordered. "Seemed dead keen on an ocean voyage," said the steward. "Sat there in his lap robe, gazing out over the rail as if he were on a tropical cruise. Seemed happy as a lark, in spite of the fact the weather was so foul the captain was considering lashing the lifeboats down. I'm convinced he didn't know what cruel fate was in store for him."

"Thank you, Cummings," said the captain. "Have the next one sent in, will you?"

Fräulein Reiter, the governess, gazed at us through her spectacles. They made her eyes appear unusually large. They looked like large, blank, silvery coins. I shuddered, thinking of coins on dead men's eyes. Really, the murder must have put me in a morbid frame of mind, I thought.

Fräulein Reiter spoke with a German accent, but with the confident, polished tones of an educated European.

"Yes. I was taking the children for their walk. There is really no proper exercise for them aboard ship, so I make a point of taking them around the deck several times in the morning, whatever the weather. This young man who has been killed, yes, I remember him. He was sitting in his chair. Really, I would not have noticed him, but the children rushed toward him and began to disturb him. They are much too open with strangers, these children. I sent them away from him, and apologized to this gentleman. He was most courteous.''

Fräulein Reiter gave a little nod, as if reenacting a moment of courtesy. "Then later I saw him asleep. At least I assumed he was asleep. It is perhaps that he was dead. I am extremely grateful that the children were not aware of this tragedy."

"And of course it is important not to upset the little ones," soothed the judge. "But do you think you could see your way to letting us talk to them for just a moment? I assure you we won't frighten them. It is important that we speak to everybody who was on deck.''

"But of course," said Fräulein Reiter. "Naturally, in an official inquiry, we must all do our duty and assist. I will send the children.''

Eight-year-old Master Bobby Fitzhugh, wiry and blond, with short trousers, scabby knees, sagging socks, and scuffed shoes, plunged into his testimony with very little coaxing. "My sister and I talked to the dead gentleman. We really did. My airplane landed on him. It's a Fokker. We went to fetch it, and talked to him. Did you take fingerprints off the knife? I bet there aren't any. Murderers always wear gloves. I want to be a detective when I grow up. Fräulein Reiter told us not to annoy him, but he didn't seem annoyed at all. I asked him if he'd like to see my stamps. I collect stamps. And then he tried to fool my sister, and make as if his thumb was cut off. You know, you bend the thumb . . .''

Here Bobby demonstrated, with some difficulty, a sleight-of-hand maneuver that gives the impression the tip of the thumb is being lifted off.

"I know how that trick works, so I wasn't fooled, but my sister began to cry. She's very little, so I'm not supposed to expect her to be as brave as I am. But, anyway, the gentleman was sorry for frightening her. He really didn't mean to. Then Fräulein Reiter came and said we weren't to annoy grown-ups. And so we went away."

"Was Fräulein Reiter with you the whole time?" asked the colonel.

"Oh, yes, she's always with us. Always," said Bobby with solemnity. "Sometimes we run ahead, but she's always there. Except at home, when we go outdoors to play, and down to visit cook and things. Our last nanny said she had eyes in the back of her head, and I was much smaller then, so I believed her, and I used to look for them in her hair, but now I know better."

"You didn't run ahead when she spoke to the gentleman, then?" continued the colonel.

"No, we were right there. I was explaining the thumb trick to Agnes, because she was still crying. And then we all went on. What will you do when you find the murderer? Will you make him walk the plank?"

"No, I'm afraid not," said the captain. "We'll hold him until we reach Canada, and then turn him over to the police there.

Bobby looked disappointed.

"They have mounties in Canada," said the judge enthusiastically. "With bright red coats, and great big horses. They'll solve the case. You'll like 'em, son. And you know, Bobby, they have a saying up there in Canada. 'The mounties always get their man.' "

Bobby seemed slightly cheered. "I have a picture of a mountie in my book on the *Many Lands of Empire*," he said.

"Now, young man," continued the judge, "who else was on the deck when you took your morning walk?"

"I *knew* you'd ask that," he cried triumphantly. "So I made a list this morning." He fished in his pocket and came up with a smudgy square of paper folded many times.

"Good lad," said the colonel approvingly. He took Bobby's list, skimmed it, and handed it to me for inclusion in the report. "The pope" I imagined was the cardinal. I was no doubt "a lady with orange hair," the piano player was probably a "dark man who didn't smile," the professor was

probably "a man with a beard." Bobby had noted here that
he suspected the beard was a false one. "A man who looks
like my uncle Wallace" was no doubt the colonel. Here,
Bobby had attached a drawing of a moon face with a
moustache, not at all unlike the colonel.

Bobby was sent to bring in his sister.

She was a child of about six, and exceedingly nervous.

"Now, then," barked the colonel officially. "You're Agnes
Fitzhugh then. Right? Speak up, child."

Agnes looked up at the colonel's fierce red face and burst
into tears. The judge glared at Colonel Marris.

"There, there, dear," I said gently. "We don't want you to
be frightened. We just want to know about the man. The man
in the deck chair. Remember? Bobby's airplane landed on
him."

Agnes stopped crying, and I smiled encouragingly. "His
finger was broken off, but it was only pretend," she said, and
began to twist a strand of her hair. "Bobby's airplane went
on him, and he gave it back. Fräulein said we mustn't annoy
him." She paused. "Is there any bread and jam?"

"No, Agnes, not here. Perhaps later Fräulein Reiter will
arrange for some. Do you remember anything more about
the man?"

"He took his nap. I take naps, too. Fräulein Reiter tucks
me in, and I sleep. But Bobby gets up again," she said darkly.

"I'm sure you're a very good girl, Agnes," I said.

"Yes," she said simply. "I am."

Fräulein Reiter came to fetch Agnes, and the colonel
shuffled through his papers. "Let's see, this musician
fellow's next. Paul Stafford. Know anything about him, captain?"

"No. The line hires these orchestras. We've had this lot for
several crossings now. Don't care too much for this ragtime
or whatever it's called, but the orchestra leader, Mr. Dixon,
is the ne'er-do-well nephew of one of our directors, so there
it is." He sighed.

"Give me a proper, old-fashioned orchestra anytime," harrumphed the colonel.

"Oh, well. These young folks must be kept amused," said the judge. "Let's see this guy."

The piano player, whose name was apparently Paul Stafford, came in and sat down.

"We understand you were on deck yesterday morning around the time this tragedy must have occurred," began the judge.

"That's right," he said.

"Talk to the murdered man? Notice him at all?"

"I noticed him. In his deck chair. Didn't talk to him, though."

"Who else did you spot on deck?"

"This young lady," he said, fixing his blue eyes on me. They were a strange, keen blue in startling contrast to his dark complexion.

"Miss Cooper, yes. And who else?"

"I didn't really notice anyone else," he said. "Oh, yes, that pale woman. The actress."

"Actress indeed," said the professor bitterly.

The judge looked as if he wanted to strike the professor. He opened his mouth as if to say something, thought better of it, and resumed the questioning.

"Anyone else?"

"I saw this man here." He pointed at the professor. "I remember him because he seemed to be mumbling to himself. It drew attention to him. It occurred to me later that might be some sign of criminal lunacy."

"Mumbling is not a sign of criminal lunacy," stated the professor with authority. "And I wasn't mumbling." We all turned to look at him, and under our collective scrutiny, his long white hands fluttered nervously over his beard. "That is, perhaps I was going over my lecture, composing my thoughts. I am adding some new material. Perhaps I was going over it in my mind . . . yes, I remember this young man. I passed him as he stood by the rail speaking to Miss Cooper. If he has taken some dislike to me without knowing me, it is probably because I remind him of someone in his past. His father, perhaps."

"I hope," interrupted Paul Stafford, addressing the group as a whole, "that you find the person responsible for this outrage. Believe me, I am well aware of the gravity of this cold-blooded murder."

Had Paul Stafford and the peculiar Professor Probrislow never met? Why had Paul said, "I hate that man"? I disregarded the professor's explanation. They didn't resemble each other at all, and, besides, what I had heard of psychology and Dr. Freud's theories impressed me as so much foolish drivel. The fad, I was sure, would pass quickly. I didn't like the professor much myself; something about his manner irritated me, but there was no reason Paul Stafford should hate the man on sight. I decided to tackle the piano player later, and find out why he had said what he had. I rather looked forward to any confrontation I might have with him. His arrogance simply cried out for some response. And my curiosity was piqued by his nervousness.

"If there are no more questions," he said in his low, silky voice, with a little tremble to it, "I will go." He rose and left the room. Somehow, his exit managed to make those of us who remained in the room feel as if we had been dismissed.

The questioning of the cardinal was facilitated by the professor, who spoke some Italian. The judge and the colonel took turns shouting questions in English, in hopes that volume alone would penetrate the barrier of language. The professor then translated into Italian. The cardinal would respond lengthily in that tongue, with a great many gestures and much eye rolling, and the professor would render these remarks into monosyllabic replies in English.

"He knows nothing," said the professor. "He remembers

seeing you, Colonel Marris, and Miss Cooper here, and the Comte de Lanier on deck. He was still on deck when the steward discovered the body."

"That's right." I nodded. "He was administering last rites or something."

"What is the purpose of your trip?" shouted the judge.

"He is traveling to New York on church business," translated the professor after a time.

"Ask him why he is traveling alone," continued the colonel suspiciously. "Don't they go about with others? Seems to me, by the look of this chap's costume, he's one of the higher-ups in the Roman church. Shouldn't he have a few ordinary padres kissing his ring and whatnot?"

A long discussion followed, during which the cardinal wept into a handkerchief bordered with wide bands of lace.

"His entourage went ahead. The cardinal missed the earlier sailing, as he was visiting a dying sister," explained the professor.

Judge Griffin said, "Aw, isn't that a shame," and patted the cardinal's hand sympathetically. The cleric composed himself, and stopped weeping.

"Somehow I can't imagine him plunging a knife into anyone's back," said the colonel. "Looks more like a Borgia poisoner type, if you ask me." The cardinal nodded and smiled, revealing a great deal of gold in his teeth.

"Amazing dental work these people have," continued the colonel. "Thank you, your eminence," he bellowed.

"*Grazie, grazie, addio,*" chorused the judge, phrases I imagined he'd picked up at the opera.

The doctor was scheduled next, and I was eager to hear the medical testimony.

His puffiness was less evident today, but he looked nervous, and held a cigarette in a trembling hand.

"Took a turn round after breakfast," he stammered. "Who did I notice? Let's see. Miss Cooper here. The children with the German governess. Mostly stood at the rail and looked out. Can't say I noticed Twist.

"Steward came and fetched me around ten-thirty. Said he was dead. Imagined the usual thing. Heart goes after the excitement of setting out on a trip. I've seen plenty of those cases. But this chap was too young for that.

"The colonel here drew my attention to a knife, firmly jabbed into the center of the back beneath the twelfth rib. Death must have been immediate. Went right through the heart at a sharp, upward angle."

"How much strength would be needed?" asked the judge.

"The trick was in the angle. Killer chose just the right angle. Any man could have done it, or even a strong woman. Very neatly done."

"Would the victim have cried out?"

"Maybe a low moan. And, of course, the wind was gusting. Even a cry would have been muffled by the wind. I tend to think it happened too fast for a cry, though."

"What can you tell us about the man from his remains?" inquired the colonel. "Occupation, that sort of thing. Any tattoos or other identifying marks?"

"Reasonably fit. Anywhere from twenty-five to thirty-two or thereabouts. The odd scar here and there. Nothing really wrong with him, other than a nasty case of dandruff. Probably fairly sedentary. Very ordinary chap. Except, of course, for the knife in his back."

I noticed a slight twitch around the doctor's left eye. He raised his hand to his temple. "There's nothing I could have done for him. He was dead when the steward found him."

"Yes, yes," said the judge. "Can you fix a time of death?"

"Rigor hadn't begun to set in when I brought him into my surgery. The body was warm even though it was pretty nippy out there. Can't imagine why he sat out there in that damned cold and wind. Blood was congealed when I found him. I haven't done any postmortem work since my student days. I'm not a police surgeon, but I'd say he couldn't have been dead very long. It could have been as little as twenty minutes. We found him at ten-thirty."

"The weapon itself," said the colonel. "I imagine it's still in your surgery?"

"Yes, as a matter of fact, it's still in Mr. Twist. Didn't see much point in disturbing it further. The authorities might prefer it that way. It's a ship's paper knife. One of these long brass things we've got lying about. It's a fairly effective weapon. Not what I'd choose, but it's still got a pretty wicked edge on it, and it's solid enough. No chance of it buckling against bone or muscle."

The captain paled. "Yes, yes, quite," he murmured.

The doctor ground out his cigarette, knocking the ashtray over. "Clumsy. So sorry. My nerves, I . . . I tell you, I have to admit it's given me a turn. I've never had to deal with much more than seasickness and an occasional case of porthole thumb, I . . ." He laughed nervously and left.

"He had a good point," said the colonel after the doctor had left. "Why was Twist sitting out there? The weather was ghastly."

"I expect," I said, after a moment of puzzled silence, "that he thought it was what one did on board ship. I mean, he was so eager to travel, in a childish way, he may have decided to do everything as he imagined it should be done. Ordering Bovril, for instance, right after breakfast. It was as if he planned everything to be as it was in the brochures. You know, when I saw him, he didn't even seem to notice the weather."

"Yes," said the captain thoughtfully, "I see what the young lady means. Some of our passengers are so keen. Playing shuffleboard in a gale and all agog about the fancy dress ball. Somehow, the inexperienced traveler often tries to accomplish everything he imagines one does on board ship. He's imagined an ideal crossing, gleaned from the travel folders, and sets out to make it happen."

"I suppose anyone on deck should explain their presence in such inclement weather," said the professor nervously. "I, for one, saw fit to seek fresh air. I find it most helpful when I'm feeling—" He broke off and eyed Colonel Marris warily.

The colonel gave him a withering look. "Feeling rum, were you? Absolutely unnecessary. All a matter of discipline. Never been seasick in my life. Never allowed myself to be." He snorted contemptuously.

"The English, no doubt, have cast-iron stomachs," said the professor in his defense.

"I don't know," mused the captain, his handsome brow wrinkled in concentration. "It's a subject to which I've given a great deal of thought. Lord Nelson, for instance, was often seasick."

"He was afraid of dogs, too," said the colonel contemptuously.

"If you were feeling so fit, and not in need of fresh air, why were you on deck?" demanded Professor Probrislow of the colonel, who was now snorting at Admiral Nelson.

"Don't trust a man who doesn't trust a dog. What's that? Why was I on deck? I take a walk every morning after breakfast. Always have, even in the Tropics. Part of my regime. Settles the stomach. Never miss my morning tramp. 'Course, it's not the same without a dog or two at one's side."

The captain coughed. "I believe Lord Nelson was not overly fond of mastiffs. I've never heard he had any strong feelings about other breeds."

I decided to wrench the conversation back to the topic at hand. "I was on deck for the same reasons as Professor Probrislow. Sorry, colonel, we aren't all as fortunate as you are in the seasickness department. And Miss Nadi has already told us she loves the sea at its wildest. The governess said she felt the children should always have a stroll, and the doctor looked unwell. Perhaps he, too, believes in the fresh air remedy." The colonel had stopped harrumphing, so I finished the list of passengers. "The cardinal, who knows, he may have been marveling at the wonder of God's sea. I can't think why the count and the piano player were out on deck. Although the piano player looks like a brooder. You know, Byronic type."

"Let's make a note to ask the piano chap what he was doing on deck in that squall," said the colonel. "Something strange about the fellow." He tapped a pencil impatiently on the table. "Wish we knew more about this Twist fellow. Keen traveler, eh? I must say, professor, you knew little about him when you hired him on. Rather unusual, isn't it? I don't like it that all his clothes were new, and his passport was, too."

"He told me he'd never traveled before," I interjected.

"There, you see," said the colonel. "This young lady knows more about him than you do."

The professor placed the tips of his fingers together and leaned back in his chair, as if about to make some great pronouncement. Smoke from his cigarette curled up from the ashtray in front of him, wreathing his face in blue. "I have a certain opinion about this young man, it is true." He favored us with a toothy smile, apparently meant to indicate candor. "To be honest, I wished to find out whatever I could about him from other sources before I spoke frankly, but as the authorities in England have wired that they are puzzled about him, perhaps it is the appropriate time to air my, er, suspicions.

"You see"—he leaned back in a professorial manner—"in my country, we are very reverent toward the dead. So I have withheld my thoughts about the young man. I wanted to give him the, how do you say, benefit of the doubt."

Professor Probrislow now leaned forward intently, forming a fist with his bony hand and pounding it on the table before him. "I think he was a criminal." He waited a moment for this to sink in. "He had all the mannerisms, all the earmarks of the habitual criminal. A furtive manner, a trem-

bling of the hands, a certain ingeniousness. I had planned to
study him at close quarters and to test my theories. I was
eager to engage him, because I saw in Mr. Twist the perfect
subject for observation, and even"—he paused dramatically
—"subtle experimentation."

"I see," said the captain, after an awkward silence. I
imagined the gentlemen on the committee were as repulsed
as I was at the cold-bloodedness of the professor somehow
experimenting on Mr. Twist. "Perhaps we should wire London again, and ask if the deceased fits the description of any
known criminals."

"Probably be a waste of time," snorted the colonel. "Very
ordinary description. Medium height, medium build. Medium everything. Brown hair. Blue eyes. Besides," he added
irritably, "the professor's basis for suspicion seems rather
vague."

The professor sighed heavily. "I have been, perhaps, too
dedicated to my science. Let us suppose he was a criminal. I
brought him into a milieu where he had the opportunity to
become a blackmailer, thereby causing his own death, his
own horrible death. . . ." He trailed off, pulling at his
strange, spiky hair.

"Blackmailers can operate anywhere," said the colonel
matter-of-factly. "You are quite sure, professor, that you
were not unintentionally aiding a criminal in flight?"

Professor Probrislow threw up his hands, obviously
alarmed. "Very well, gentlemen, I'll be frank. Although what
I am about to tell you may seem odd to the unscientific
mind. That is why I was at first reluctant to tell you. But I
see now I must be frank."

"Good," said the captain.

The professor ignored the implied criticism of his previous behavior. "Yes, I knew he was a criminal. In fact, he had
been a blackmailer. But he was not in flight. He was recently
released from prison. I took him on to see if he was capable
of mending his ways. And I wanted to study a criminal out-

side of a prison. So much of our work is hampered by the lack of opportunity to observe criminals going about their business, without bars and chains."

"Why haven't you told us this before?" demanded the captain. "This is murder, man. Nothing to trifle with."

The professor fiddled with his cigarette case. He didn't answer.

"Well, if Mr. Twist was a blackmailer," said the judge, "our task is unpleasant. We must find everyone on board with something to hide." There was a gleam in his eye that indicated he thought the task might not be altogether unpleasant.

"Horrors," said the captain. "I'd rather leave that to the Canadian authorities. We mustn't upset the passengers. It could be very sticky."

"It could be dangerous," said the colonel.

"Cheer up, gentlemen," said Judge Griffin. "At least we've found ourselves a motive."

There was a tap at the door.

CHAPTER FIVE

"Ah, Hawkins," said the captain. I recognized our cabin steward, a coarse-featured man with lanky blond hair and a rough, ruddy complexion.

"Begging your pardon, captain. I thought I should bring you this straightaway. I didn't bring it with the gentleman's things this morning, because it was found later, when the room was done up. On the washstand it was, sir." He handed over a ring with a large blue stone. "I wouldn't want you to think I hadn't brought it round straightaway," he added smarmily.

"Very well, Hawkins," said the captain. "I'm sure your honesty is not at question here."

"Thank you, captain." Hawkins lingered at the door. "Didn't bring him much luck, now, did it?"

"Luck?" queried the colonel.

"That's right. Said it was supposed to bring him luck, the young gentleman did."

"Thank you, Hawkins," said the captain firmly. "You may go." He examined the ring. "We'll put this with the other things."

"May I see it?" asked the colonel. "Hmm. This is quite old, I'd wager. Unlike the poor lad's clothes and luggage. Looks like lapis lazuli. And what's this, carved into the back of the stone? I believe it's a peacock."

We heard a ruckus in the vestibule, and the throaty tones of Vera Nadi. "I tell you, I must speak to the captain. I have something important to tell him."

The door burst open. Miss Nadi, preceded by a powerful

61

scent, which I decided was jasmine, burst into the room. "This blackmailer, I know now that my suspicions—"

She stopped, stared at the ring as Colonel Marris held it up to the light, let out a contralto scream, and fell into a swoon.

The judge rushed to her side. "The doctor at once!" he cried. "What should we do?" Miss Nadi had sunk into his arms, still except for a barely perceptible flutter of her dark lashes.

"I believe," said the captain delicately, "that her stays must be loosened."

"Good heavens, we don't wear stays anymore," I snapped. "Put her feet higher than her heart."

They all looked alarmed. "Here," I said, grabbing a cushion. "Put her feet on this and let her down gently. She'll come around soon, and then we should give her some mild stimulant. A cup of tea or something."

"Have you any brandy?" said Colonel Marris to the captain.

"Yes," I said, "just the thing."

Miss Nadi opened her dark, liquid eyes and held out a pale hand. "Yes, just a drop," she murmured. "The shock . . ."

The captain rummaged in his desk and came up with a square decanter and a small glass. I filled the glass and held it to her lips.

"Ah, thank you. If I could just sit for a moment."

The judge helped her to a chair.

"If you feel it coming on again," I said firmly, "put your head between your knees."

"May we know," asked the colonel politely, "what brought on this spell?"

"I—I see now," she said softly, her eyes narrowing. She seemed to be speaking to the professor. "Please summon maid. When I am stronger, I shall speak of this again. I'm not sure . . ." She trailed off.

"You seemed to recognize this." The colonel placed the ring in her hand.

She smiled wanly. "Yes, I think I do." She examined it closely. The ornate setting was of reddish gold, and the large oval stone was a deep, opaque blue.

"The ring," said the professor, "belongs to me. You must be mistaken, madame. The strain of the murder, your anxiety over the blackmailer, these anxieties, they all come together, and your unconscious mind focuses them all on this harmless little object. I am an alienist. I know the human mind can play these tricks. If you like, we can discuss this in depth later. You will find it, I'm sure, a very profitable discussion." He smiled, revealing pointed canines. "I suggest for now a mild sedative. Perhaps the doctor can . . ."

Miss Nadi tossed down the remaining brandy, rose, and left as abruptly as she had arrived.

"Will she be okay?" asked the judge, obviously concerned.

"She is sturdier than she appears," replied Professor Probrislow coldly.

"What do you know about this ring, professor?" demanded Colonel Marris. Unobtrusively, I resumed my note-taking.

The professor gave out with another of his extravagant sighs. "It will seem peculiar, I realize. The boy, Twist, he was so nervous about this trip. He had fears of drowning. He had, it seems, a cousin on the *Titanic*."

The captain shuddered, and the professor continued. "He was irrational, so I used an irrational means to quiet him. I told him to wear this ring, that it would protect him, that in my country a blue stone such as this was a talisman against accidental death. He believed me, and seemed eager to wear the ring. Criminals—and he was of the criminal class—are a superstitious lot. It seemed harmless enough."

Nobody said anything, perhaps because the story seemed so farfetched.

"Well, you must admit it was less conspicuous than a wreath of garlic," said the professor feebly.

"Won't wash," said Colonel Marris.

The professor turned an unlikely shade of pink and said, "I know it sounds silly. But I was testing him; I already told you I meant to test my theories on him. I wanted to see if—"

"If he were honest?" said the colonel dryly. "Like the housewife who puts a shilling under the mat to see if the parlormaid will discover it and return it?"

"That's the general idea," said the professor feebly. "May I have the ring back, please? I'll give you a receipt for it." He seemed to gather himself together again, and said, quite firmly, "I would like it back."

"And you shall have it back," said the captain, "after we dock in Montreal and the authorities are finished with it."

He smiled a social smile at the professor, who muttered, "Very well."

"Let's have the next passenger in," said Judge Griffin, rubbing his hands together and smoothly glossing over an awkward moment.

Jack Clancy burst in energetically. He looked very dapper in a vivid collegiate sweater and plus fours. "All I want to know," said Mr. Clancy enthusiastically, "is why Vera Nadi strolled out of here with a shot glass and the urge to kill. She didn't seem to want to kill me, either, which is what she wanted to do when she came in."

"We'll ask the questions, if you don't mind," said the captain in a pleasant voice. "So you're the reporter Miss Nadi told us about."

"Must be," said Professor Probrislow. "She mentioned specifically that he had a square jaw."

Jack Clancy ran a hand over his jaw. "Well, I suppose it is," he said. "And a good thing, too. I'd hate to have to hide a weak chin under a beard. What's your chin like, professor?"

"Have you been bothering Miss Nadi?" inquired the judge before the professor had a chance to answer.

"It's open season on moving picture stars," replied Jack Clancy casually, lighting in the chair before us.

"We're talking about blackmail," thundered Judge Griffin, his gothic eyebrows drawn menacingly together.

"I'm just doing a job, your honor. I make my living telling it all to an eager public. The best, the worst, all of it but the dull parts. Why should I turn down a scoop for a few bucks in a private blackmail scheme when I make a pretty good living blabbing it all to the world?"

The captain shuddered at Mr. Clancy's description of journalism, and said, "Miss Nadi wondered if you hadn't threatened her with an unflattering story if she didn't give you an interview. And there was more serious blackmail as well."

Mr. Clancy now threw back his head and laughed heartily. "Is that what she said? That I was blackmailing her? Why, she'd be playing her scenes to the strains of the piano in the parlor one flight down if it weren't for guys like me. These movie stars need publicity to survive in the game, and she knows it.

"Not that I enjoy this sob-sister stuff," he added in a more serious vein. "But when I fall over a story, I've got to cover it. You see, I am really"—he stood up now, summoning all his dignity—"a *sportswriter*."

Suddenly Mr. Clancy seemed very young to me. I suppressed a giggle; he shot me a look, seemed surprised to find himself standing, and sat down again. "Blackmail, eh?" he said thoughtfully.

"Miss Nadi has been bothered by something of the sort," said the colonel offhandedly.

"Think it fits in with the murder?" asked Jack Clancy eagerly.

"May we ask you a few questions?" said the colonel.

"Of course," Clancy replied. "I hope I can help."

"Why are you traveling on this vessel? Where have you been and where are you going?"

"I've been in London, covering the Parkinson-Dorrity fight for the *San Francisco Globe*. Dorrity's a hometown boy, you know. It was quite a fight. And I followed up a lead on Judge Crater. I had four tips placing him in London. But nothing came of it. I'm on my way home."

"Did you know the victim, Mr. Twist?" asked Judge Griffin.

"No. Didn't notice him, either. Until he met his dramatic end. What do you know about him?"

"Very little. Were you on deck yesterday morning?" inquired the colonel.

"Mystery man, eh? Shipboard victim, man without a past."

"Please," said the colonel impatiently, "answer the question."

"Yes, I took a turn around the deck. In pursuit of the elusive Miss Nadi. Missed the killing altogether, worse luck. Rather neat bit of work, eh, gentlemen? Quick, clean, almost professional, I'd say."

"Professional?" said Probrislow, raising an eyebrow.

"I spent some time on the police beat. Seen a few stiffs in my time. This looked pretty neat to me."

"You've examined the corpse?" asked the colonel.

Jack Clancy smiled amiably. "And my editor called this trip a junket. Sure, the Judge Crater thing was a phony, but the fight was a terrific fight. And now I've got my hands completely full. Exclusive Vera Nadi interview, deck chair stabbing mystery, and the Comte de Lanier's good for a line or two. He's going to marry Marjorie Klepp, the Michigan cotter-pin heiress. Our readers love that stuff.

"And let me give you fellows a tip. The count's probably not what he appears to be. Old man Klepp's being taken for a ride. 'Heiress Bowled Over by No-Account Count.' How's that sound? I'm working that angle, anyway. Looks promising.

"Say, listen." Mr. Clancy rose and sat cozily on the oak table in front of us. "I'd be glad to cooperate with you in any

way I can. And in exchange, of course, I'd appreciate getting
what I can from you. You know, inside stuff, for my readers.
Think about it. I'll be investigating this stabbing business
anyway. We may as well share and share alike. After all, you
need the killer, I need a story. And besides," he added airily,
"I don't like to see harmless little secretaries get stabbed to
death in deck chairs. It isn't right."

"Whom did you see on deck?" inquired Colonel Marris
firmly.

Clancy produced a brown pigskin notebook. "The cardinal, two kids and their grim-visaged governess, the alleged
count, and, of course, my quarry, Miss Nadi. She really does
want to give me an interview. She's just being coy."

"It seems fruitless to prevent Mr. Clancy from making his
own inquiries," said the professor after the reporter had
left, at first refusing to relinquish his passport "to anybody
who isn't an American official," then finally turning it over
to Judge Griffin.

"Heck, these newsboys aren't so bad, Marris," said the
judge, flipping through the passport. "He sure does have a
square jaw. Take a look at this picture."

We all observed Mr. Clancy's portrait, and the professor
began, "Very interesting what Lombroso says about jaws."

Judge Griffin cut him off. "Doesn't hurt to play ball with
the press once in a while."

"I find Mr. Clancy's manner most unbecoming," said the
captain prissily. "I shudder to think of his annoying the
passengers."

"He must be restrained," hissed Professor Probrislow. "I
don't like the shape of the man's face. Lombroso says—"

Colonel Marris interrupted. "How did he get a gander at
the corpse, I wonder? Remarkable chap. Certainly one of the
breezier Americans. Clancy. Irish blood. Hmm."

"That's easy," said the judge. "I saw the doctor and this
Clancy fellow tossing down a few before lunch. Mrs. Griffin

doesn't hold with drinking before lunch"—he winked—"but I stepped into the smoking room for a cigar. Clancy was getting pretty chummy with your sawbones."

"I've spoken to Chambers about his drinking," said the captain, wincing. "Mind you, he's a perfectly sound man. Knows his stuff."

"Think Clancy's a blackmailer?" asked the judge.

"He's free with the stuff of his trade if he is," said the colonel. "If the count is not what he seems, it should be good for a considerable sum."

"That's right," said the judge indignantly. "I'm sure the Klepps would call the whole thing off if they knew the count was a phony. Why, that lousy gigolo!" he exclaimed.

"So what," sneered the professor. "Miss Klepp's blood is not blue."

"Please, gentlemen," said the captain calmly. "It is not for us to determine whether or not the count's pedigree is in order. Let us confine ourselves to information that seems to apply to the crime at hand."

"Just in case this guy is the real thing, what do we call him?" asked the judge, before the arrival of the Comte de Lanier. "My lord?" His voice rose a little in eager anticipation.

" 'Count' will do," said the captain.

The count slouched aristocratically into the room. He did have, I mused, a magnificently noble nose. He wore a fawn-colored coat over his shoulder and carried pearl glacé kid gloves and a handsome gold-knobbed stick. On closer scrutiny, I decided the stick was perhaps a trifle too ornate.

The count's memory was sketchy indeed. He remembered seeing no one. After some prompting, he acknowledged my presence, and Miss Nadi's.

"And I know nothing of this person Twist," he said with finality. "I hope that this will be all. I am most pressed to continue my journey. I hope it will not be that I must remain after the ship has docked. Why this man must have been killed as I was promenading myself, I do not know." The count took the attitude that Mr. Twist had done this expressly to annoy him.

"Yes, yes," said the judge affably. "I understand, count, that you're on your way to America to marry." He paused. "One of our beautiful American girls."

The count nodded stiffly.

"A very rich American girl," added the colonel. I was shocked. There was an uncomfortable pause, and the count reddened. He looked as if he were about to say something, but couldn't decide what it should be. The colonel leaned over the table, eyeing the count, reminding me of a bulldog.

"See here, Marris," murmured the captain.

"There may be a blackmailer on board," said the colonel. "The count should know this. Impersonation of European nobility is not unknown on American shores."

"Sir," said the count, throwing down a glove. "You have, I see, the insolence of the English. How dare you question my authenticity, indeed, my antecedents?"

"I'm afraid we must be thorough," said the colonel briskly. "After all, we have a murderer on board."

"Surely it is not I you accuse!" shrieked the count.

"I'm not accusing anybody. But it is for your own protection that I warn you that an odious blackmailer may be among us," said the colonel.

The count calmed himself somewhat. "You are mistaken about me," he said. "Many records were destroyed by the Revolution. I have a claim, a legitimate claim to my title, unlike the shopkeepers of the Second Empire, the children of Robespierre, who so eagerly pretended royal blood after they had spilled so much themselves." He held his head back proudly. His nostrils were arched, and he surveyed us from beneath half-lowered lids. He snatched up his glove and left.

"Pretty rough on him, weren't you, Marris?" asked the judge. "I think he's the real thing. Clancy's on the wrong track. He's gotta be genuine."

Colonel Marris and the captain returned this opinion with a piteous glance.

"Most unlikely," said the professor. "His bearing is all wrong. Undoubtedly nothing but an adventurer. Ah, well, what will it matter to Miss Klepp in any case?" He examined his fingernails.

The judge looked troubled. He was undoubtedly struggling with twin American instincts: a love of democracy and a fascination with European nobility. He waved a hand in the air, and said in an irritated voice, "Ah, hell, the guy's probably real."

But I resolved to find out what I could for myself, and, because the committee had finished its work for the day, I went to the ship's library. There I found the auburn-haired conductress. What this lady actually did was a mystery to me. The passenger list advised that ladies traveling alone could arrange for an interview with the ship's conductress, but what the content of the interview was intended to be, I couldn't imagine.

"Oh, Miss Cooper," she said eagerly. I wondered if she intended to swoop me away for a mysterious interview. "I'm selecting some books for Mrs. Destinoy-Pinchot. Some of our more exclusive passengers seldom emerge from their cabins at all," she added. That was a point against the count, I decided. "Most unnatural, I think, but if they are more comfortable that way . . ."

I inquired as to the availability of the *Almanach de Gotha*. "Oh yes," she chirped. "We have quite a few reference works here. The gentlemen so often use them to settle wagers. Not that I hold with gambling. I've seen some dreadful things. People have been ruined at the bridge table in a single crossing. People are often not themselves at sea," she added darkly. "I try to be a steadying influence when I can. Ah, here it is."

I sat in a quiet corner, consulting the heavy volume.

"No, the Comte de Lanier's not in there," said Mr. Clancy, who had joined me silently, giving me rather a turn. He stood before me, running the brim of his cap through his large hands.

"You startled me," I said, annoyed.

"I already checked," he continued. " 'Course, I won't have a really good story till I discover who he really is. 'Madcap Heiress Weds Defrocked Priest,' now that'd be a story. Somehow, though, I think he might be a hairdresser. What do you think?"

"I thought you didn't like the sob-sister stuff," I said coolly.

"It *is* sickening, isn't it?" He sighed, and sat down beside me. "When I'm not looking for Judge Crater, I really am a sportswriter. Now that's writing; that's real writing. Good training for the novel I'll write some day. But as long as the *Globe* is paying the rent, I'm honor-bound to give 'em my best. Say . . . how'd you get into the inner sanctum, anyhow?" he demanded.

"I take shorthand," I replied. "I hated studying it, but Father insisted. Said he didn't want a lot of sour-faced women around, or ambitious young men, and that he wanted me to help him with his business. He's in the wholesale hardware business."

"Sounds fascinating," said Mr. Clancy unconvincingly. "Think the committee's on to anything? It's gotta be the blackmail angle. Twist must have been putting the squeeze on someone. That's why he was killed."

I shrugged and tried to look noncommittal.

" 'Course, the Nadi woman thinks I'm the blackmailer." He chuckled. "It doesn't figure. Why would anybody advertise themselves as a blackmail victim? A cheap publicity stunt, that's what it is. You know what gets my goat?" he continued. "She says I probably sent her the damned note, and she won't tell me what's in it." He laughed heartily.

That did seem unfair. I decided to give Mr. Clancy a hint. " 'Everything I have done has been for love,' " I repeated in Miss Nadi's dramatic tones.

Jack Clancy laughed. "Hey, that's pretty good. Any idea who he was? I mean, the note must have threatened to expose a particular, er, liaison."

"A certain noble personage," I continued in Miss Nadi's accents, and we both laughed.

He looked serious for a second. "Say, that reminds me of a story the judge told the other night. It'd be a coincidence, but—let me see, what was the name of that country?"

"Graznia?" I said softly. I enjoyed watching Jack unravel what he could. I felt justified in bringing forth the name, as he'd already made the connection between Vera Nadi and the judge's story. I should have felt guilty, I suppose, for being so indiscreet, but it occurred to me I'd never discover what Mr. Clancy knew if I didn't volunteer some information of my own. And the Nadi story seemed the least critical information to offer. After all, the judge had blathered his story around, and Miss Nadi herself seemed to bring attention to her blackmail note. Neither did she show any reticence at revealing the substance of the scandal.

"Yeah," said Jack. "One of those Balkan places full of brigands and impassable mountains. Graznia. Didn't it disappear after the war, along with Herzegovena, Bosnia, Serbia and Montenegro?"

He flipped through the *Almanach de Gotha* beside us. "Let's see, Graznia. House of Crespi-Gravenstein, page three ninety-eight." He leafed through the pages, but page 398 was missing. It had been very carefully removed.

Mr. Clancy let out a long, low whistle.

"We must tell someone on the committee," I said.

He shrugged. "Okay. Let's see what they say."

We found Colonel Marris on deck, leaning against the rail, squinting out to sea, pipe in hand. "Cut clean out, you say? Hmmm. Crespi-Gravenstein. Distant cousins of his majesty,

I believe. Well, anybody could've cut it out. Thing's probably been around for donkey's years." He pushed tobacco into the bowl of his pipe with a practiced thumb.

"Graznia," murmured Clancy. "What was it I heard about the place? Before we sailed, an English newshound I met in London, he was following up on it. Said there was bound to be a spot of trouble there."

"Could be," said the colonel, fumbling for a match, "that there'll be a show there soon. Our chaps would like to keep things quiet, naturally. Can't allow another Balkan situation. Place has always been the tinderbox of Europe. Can't see what it's got to do with poor old Twist, though."

"For a little two-bit country, Graznia seems to be coming up a lot," said Mr. Clancy. "Wish I could remember what this fellow in London told me. Let's see. Something about a bunch of anarchists. Comrades of the something-or-other."

The colonel's face took on a queer expression. "The Comrades of the New Dawn," he said softly.

"Huh?" said Mr. Clancy.

The colonel looked at him carefully, and lit his pipe. "This Graznia business, it goes far beyond Miss Nadi. Whether it has anything to do with this murder or not, it's terribly important just now. More important than Mr. Twist."

"Nothing is more important than human life," I said.

The colonel glanced at me. He smiled a sad smile; it was the condescending smile of age. It seemed to say, "When you are my age, you will know differently." I stamped my foot impatiently and vowed never to smile that condescending smile, no matter how old and wise I became.

"I remember now," said Mr. Clancy. "The English reporter. He talked about these comrades trying to seize Graznia. Or turn it topsy-turvy."

The colonel sighed. "Graznia is no more, but there still remains strong national feeling among the Graznian people. They're a rough-and-tumble lot, the Graznians. Wild and hot-blooded. The nationalists have come under the sway of the

Comrades of the New Dawn. And the Comrades see Graznia as the ideal proving ground for their half-baked social theories. Very dangerous theories, too, I might add." He narrowed his eyes. "Wild lot of anarchists is what they are. Ungodly, undisciplined, unscrupulous anarchists.

"God knows why they want Graznia. It's a miserable little corner of the world. And the Comrades are a motley crew, handing out their rubbishy leaflets and holding forth in Hyde Park. But what they lack in finesse, they more than make up for in sheer fanaticism. Our chaps thought they were on to them when they rounded up one of their leaders in London. Strange sort of fellow—German mother, Brazilian father. Sigismund Salazar. Somehow got hold of a cyanide capsule." He sucked his pipe noisily. "Our chaps back at square one. Damned shame."

"Well, what's all this have to do with the murder?" I said.

The colonel smiled at me. "Nothing. Nothing apparent, in any case."

"It seems to me," said Jack, "that the only connection is through the blackmail angle. Vera Nadi claims she got a note exposing the Graznia scandal. Twist could have been a blackmailer. He put the squeeze on the Nadi dame, who doesn't seem to have minded. But, somewhere, he blackmailed somebody who did mind, and who killed him."

"And," I said, "it sounds to me like the murderer had to be someone seen on deck yesterday morning."

"Let's see," said Jack, "who would make a good blackmail victim?" He pulled out his leather-bound notebook. "The doctor?"

"Drinks," said the colonel.

"Maybe he lost a patient when he was on a bender," ventured Mr. Clancy in hopeful tones.

"The count," I continued, "might not be genuine. He certainly would have something to lose if he were exposed to the Klepps."

Jack frowned and consulted his list. "There's Miss Cooper here. But she's out, of course." He grinned at me.

"I don't know why I'm thought incapable of murder. And incapable of having a ghastly secret." I pouted.

"The children and their governess. Hardly a hotbed of secret sin there, I should imagine. Professor Probrislow," he continued. "There *is* something strange about him. But I haven't got a handle on anything worth killing for in his past. The colonel here"—Jack nodded respectfully—"appears to be thoroughly above board. Now Miss Nadi, she seems blackmail-proof. Shreds blackmail notes to pieces with her scarlet talons on a regular basis, according to her."

"Maybe," I mused, "she has a real secret. Something that is important. And the royal scandal business is a blind."

"Could be, could be," said the colonel. "Although there is very little a woman of that sort need hide. These actresses and theatrical people live by entirely different standards. That applies to the pianist as well. These artists. No shame at all."

"Somehow I can't imagine a blackmail note in English having much effect on the cardinal. And I can't imagine Twist had much Italian," said Jack.

"I suppose," I said, "he really is a cardinal?"

I waited until the colonel left us before I told Jack he was on the right track. "Don't tell them I told you," I said recklessly, "but the professor says Twist *was* a blackmailer. He'd been in jail and everything."

"So I've heard," said Jack. The man seemed to know everything.

CHAPTER SIX

*T*he next morning was the morning of the boat drill. Aunt Hermione always became somewhat agitated during boat drills. They were so closely allied in her mind with actual disaster that she half-believed the ship was going down each time she heard the whistle.

Gloomily, she surveyed our cabin as if she were viewing her belongings for the last time. There were plenty of belongings for her to bid farewell to. Aunt Hermione believed in traveling with anything that might possibly come in handy, and she believed in making one's surroundings as much like home as possible. The dressing table was cluttered with scent bottles, pincushions, jars and creams, framed photographs, and souvenirs.

I viewed it all with a shudder, almost hoping the ship *would* sink. Bric-a-brac was unsettling to me. I liked clear, clean surfaces, and whenever company came to our house, I always whisked Aunt Hermione's collection of antimacassars from the furniture. It was our only area of strong disagreement.

I hurried Aunt Hermione along. We always learned our lifeboat station first thing. Aunt Hermione felt it was a genuinely important safety measure, and I dreaded making an idiot of myself during a boat drill. I handed her one of the life vests, and we went up on deck.

We stood by the boat, the wind whipping our hair, the sky blue and the breeze bracing. Aunt Hermione always managed to hold her partridgelike figure in a somewhat military way as we waited for the captain to come around. I tried to look as relaxed as anyone could with one of those ridiculous orange life vests around one's neck, and I glanced at the other occupants of our lifeboat, should Aunt Hermione's fears come to something. Much to my chagrin, Mr. Ogle was present, making all sorts of silly jokes about being ship-wrecked.

"And Miss Cooper here can cook us up sea gull eggs, I'm sure," he twittered on.

My aunt frowned. "It's not a matter for levity, Mr. Ogle," she said sternly. "I'm shocked that you, who have apparently done so much to aid the widows and orphans of drowned sailors, should have such a cavalier attitude toward disaster at sea."

Mr. Ogle looked slightly confused, and then remembered that all his amateur shipboard theatricals were in aid of seamen's charities.

The captain strolled by, and we tried to look ready to face the worst hand fate could deal us. Aunt Hermione gazed with a brave, steely gleam past the captain out to the beauti-fully calm sea. The captain favored us all with a nod, and I thought how really handsome he looked with his strong features and unclouded brow. His beard and bearing gave him a startling resemblance to the king of England.

After he had strolled on, and we had been dismissed, Aunt Hermione touched my arm. "Iris," she exclaimed, "why there's . . ." she trailed off. "Isn't it extraordinary," she said. "I just know I've seen an old friend, but for the moment I can't imagine *who* it is. Strange how memory plays tricks with one. Of course, it could have been years ago."

"Where?" I said.

"There, the stout lady in tweeds, with the young girl. I must run through the passenger list and see if I can match the name to the face. Somehow, I remember her as much *softer*-looking."

I bobbed up and down, but couldn't see the woman Aunt

Hermione had recognized. It was amazing how often one met people one knew aboard ship. Aunt Hermione had told me many times about the terribly naive adulterous couple from Portland who booked a suite on the *Leviathan* and promptly ran into six people they knew. "Very foolish," said Aunt Hermione. "They'd been so discreet back home. Let that be a lesson to you, my dear. Not that you'll ever need to hide anything from the world. Still, if you do, for *goodness sake*, don't make such a foolish mistake."

I left Aunt Hermione stowing our life vests back under the beds and searching for the passenger list to jog her memory about the woman she'd spotted on deck. As arranged, I went back to the captain's cabin, where the committee held its final meeting.

The captain shuffled through the passports. Colonel Marris stacked sheafs of paper together; the judge and the professor looked alert and terribly official. I could only wonder what the group would do next. It occurred to me that I was no longer needed; all the testimony had been taken. Presumably, the men would now analyze the evidence. But I sat quietly, banking on the fact that people are creatures of habit. My presence was familiar now, and I hoped they wouldn't notice I was superfluous.

Colonel Marris leaned back and placed the tips of his fingers together. "Our work here, gentlemen, is finished. We have established that a limited number of people were on deck when Mr. Twist was killed. They all corroborate each others' statements. That is, everyone was seen by someone else at some time or other. Everyone took a few turns on deck at different paces. It *is* possible that someone slipped out on deck, did the deed, and slipped back, but it's not likely. There's too much deck to cross unobserved. Twist's chair was as far away from any door as possible. If Miss Cooper here and the children and the deck steward hadn't spoken to the man, I would be inclined to think his corpse had been arranged in the deck chair. But that's tricky, too. Carting a corpse around the promenade deck would be conspicuous.

"If Miss Cooper hadn't seen the fellow drinking his blasted Bovril, I'd say the deck steward might have had a crack at doing away with the poor lad. Leaned over him, stabbed him, appearing to be serving him Bovril," the colonel said.

"Unless, of course," I said, "the deck steward and I are in collusion."

To my annoyance, the judge seemed to be suppressing a smile. "Quite," said the colonel offhandedly. He frowned and sought the thread of his narrative. "Bovril. Yes. Hmm. Let me see. In any case, it was a most daring crime. True, there were few people on deck, but the killer had no way of knowing when someone would come around the corner and catch him at it. Twist's chair was partly obscured by lifeboats and so forth from various angles, but still . . . it's incredible. Almost a desperate act, yet so calculated. Knife thrust neatly into the body where it would do the most good. Or its worst, I should say."

"I am glad to think that, from what the doctor says, anyway," mused the judge, "he never knew what hit him. Well, it seems as though we have very little idea of opportunity, other than the list of people on deck. As to motive, well, blackmail's the best we've got. And it looks good to me. Shady background, perhaps a criminal past." The judge gestured toward the professor.

"Yes," said Judge Griffin, "I think the blackmail angle is our best shot. We have absolutely no other hint of possible motive. And in my experience, the most obvious solution is inevitably the correct one."

The captain cleared his throat. "I concur with the judge. But I find it most disturbing. I suggest we simply give this information to the authorities when we dock. They can peruse the list of suspects, and match the suspect with a guilty secret. No doubt the Blue Star Line will employ its own private inquiry agents as well. They'll be asking all sorts of questions. Most distressing. But we can leave it to them. We have begun the work, they can discover the guilty party." He wrung his hands. "Gentlemen, this is indeed unpleasant. It is the position of the Blue Star Line that first-class passengers do not indulge in behavior likely to draw the notice of a blackmailer. Nor do they commit murder. I suppose there is no possibility that a second-class or steerage passenger could be responsible?"

He looked pensive. "Of course, steerage is not as it was before the war. Nowadays, one has a lot of university professors and young fellows with rucksacks. But still . . ."

"Not terribly likely," said the colonel. "Everyone seems to have been accounted for. Although I suppose a passenger of another class could have penetrated into first class. Ask your stewards if they spotted anything of the kind."

"Yes, well, it was just an idea." The captain sighed. "I suppose we can return all these passports."

"No, no," said the colonel sharply. "We don't want anyone who was on deck to slip through immigration before the authorities speak to him."

"Oh, yes, I see. Well, Miss Cooper, perhaps you would like to use my office here to transcribe these notes. I will arrange to have a typewriting machine brought here."

I was disappointed. Committee of experts, indeed! I felt they should have pursued the case until they found the culprit. The men filed out, and I arranged my notes. Scanning the testimony of the professor and the colonel, laboriously rendered in the captain's old-fashioned script, I discovered very little.

Like the other passengers, they remembered several people on deck, and they had observed Twist in his deck chair. They had observed nothing out of the ordinary.

The typewriter was brought to the cabin, a shiny black Underwood, a very nice machine with an easy touch. I began rendering the notes into typed form.

I had decided that the killer had to be one of the handful of people on deck. Everyone on our list had been placed there by other witnesses, and surely anyone else would have been seen by someone. It was a strange list of people. The professor, who reminded me somehow of a lizard. Was it his skin, dry and rough, or his strange, sudden manner? The colonel, who seemed to be a typical retired military man, and a man with high standards and self-discipline—surely he led a life marked by moral rectitude; I found him an unlikely blackmail victim. Vera Nadi seemed a passionate, volatile woman, and she had, I thought, sufficient egocentricity to take another life. I remembered, too, her strange wild smile as she looked out to sea, soon after Twist must have died. She was a blackmail victim and admitted it freely—even relished it. But was she telling the truth? Or was her nonchalance covering a real fear of blackmail? The governess and children seemed unlikely assassins. And they had been together. True, there was something perhaps a little sinister about Fräulein Reiter. One sensed that beneath her reserve might lie some inner core of more fiery stuff. The piano player, Paul Stafford, worried me. I did not want him to be a murderer. Yet there was a seething passion there, a sense of mission, and he was a troubled man. The cardinal—well, it was hard to know what to think of the cardinal. The barrier of language made him into a comical character, a childish person. What he was really like, I had no idea. I remembered only too keenly how idiotic I must have seemed while struggling with fragments of a language; people had perceived me as a sympathetic lunatic. The doctor could certainly have had a disreputable past, but somehow I couldn't imagine him summoning up the nerve to commit violent murder. His nerve seemed absolutely shot, and, as a doctor, he had access to all sorts of subtler weapons, such as deadly poisons. Jack Clancy, in his abrasive way, was not without charm, although his manners were off-putting. In fact, if the truth were known, his manners were terrible. It seemed almost as if a person would have to try very hard to have such awful manners. Perhaps Jack Clancy was not a reporter at all. If he were a murderer, posing as a journalist would be very handy. It would make it easy to poke around and discover how the investigation was going without looking suspicious. Of course, Mr. Clancy was passing himself off as a newspaperman before the murder, and presumably before Mr. Twist could have blackmailed him, unless Mr. Twist blackmailed him *because* he was posing as a reporter. The Comte de Lanier, now, he was posing as something he wasn't. At least everyone thought so. Somehow, the count struck me as more the slippery, wiggly sort, who'd never find himself in such a tough spot that he'd have to kill to get out of it.

I was sorry that Mr. Twist was a blackmailer. It did seem to be true; there was no other explanation for his death. No one had any apparent connection with him, so his death could hardly have been the result of a long-standing enmity. The professor had known Twist longer than anyone, but Twist himself had told me he'd only been engaged recently.

Whatever the facts, the professor's behavior when faced with the big blue ring was certainly suspicious. The professor's story had simply not rung true. And, if the solution to the mystery hinged on the professor, Paul Stafford, the piano player, might also be involved in some way. He knew the professor. "I hate that man," he had said. Paul Stafford didn't seem to have known Twist, though. Which was a bit of a relief. I wanted Paul Stafford out of it.

Disgusted with the committee, I resolved to find out as much as I could about the professor and about Paul Stafford. It wouldn't be easy. The professor didn't seem to care for me. He had barely tolerated my presence on the committee, but then he seemed to dislike everyone. He seemed to have taken a special dislike to Vera Nadi. Most telling, I thought. Probably a disappointment in love in his past. What else would have turned him into such a bitter man?

Paul Stafford seemed equally mysterious, but he *did* care about something. Passionately. There was a dark fire there, and a sense of purpose. The intensity of the man frightened me.

I checked the typed pages for errors, and looked for clues in the testimony. It was a fruitless task. There seemed to be nothing there that pointed to anyone as the killer. Stacking the papers neatly, I discovered that I was lingering in the captain's office. Why? Perhaps because I resisted the idea of leaving the case, and of leaving it unsolved.

Suddenly Jack Clancy rushed in, without knocking, and eyed the completed transcripts greedily. I folded the sheaf of papers in two.

"Oh, come on," he said. "Let me have a look at 'em."

"I really can't," I said. "You know that. This is an official inquiry. If you have any questions, you must speak to the captain." It was hard to be firm with Mr. Clancy. He seemed like a terrier that clamped its jaw around a leg and hung on and shook. I felt sure he always got what he wanted—that he took what he wanted.

"Now, listen, the way I see it, you're as keen on getting to the bottom of this as I am. You're a sharp-witted girl, probably read lots of detective stories; you figure you're at least as smart as those fellows on the committee, right?"

"Well, really, I—"

"Well, sure you are. Now I'm getting a lot of information together. And you have some yourself. Let's pool it. My interest is purely professional, of course. All I get out of this is a by-line, but you'll have the satisfaction of having unraveled a dastardly plot and brought a heinous murderer to justice."

Jack Clancy was persuasive, but I held firm and told him that under no circumstances could I reveal the contents of the statements.

"There's really nothing there anyway," I said. "Just a lot of people who were on deck. Nobody saw anything. They just all confirm that the others were also on deck."

" 'Baffling Deck Chair Murder. Authorities Have No Clue,' " muttered Jack to himself. " 'No Witnesses to Daring Crime.' Well, if there's nothing there, why won't you let me have a look at the stuff?"

"No. No. No," I said emphatically.

Undaunted, Jack plunged on. "How come the Nadi dame needed a restorative? What happened to make her forget the complaint she was going to lodge about me?"

"She felt faint," I said.

"Yeah? What brought that on?"

"Really, Mr. Clancy! I'm not supposed to discuss—"

Jack stroked his chin. "Let's see. I was stationed outside that door all afternoon. She came in right after Hawkins showed up with the ring. Big blue thing—did you see it?"

"Yes," I said impatiently. "It belonged to Twist. Or the professor, or somebody. No, really, Mr. Clancy, I must give this to the captain, he'll attach any more information, and then it will all be sealed up until we reach Montreal. There's really nothing more to discuss."

"What's he attaching?" asked Jack.

"Just the information from the passports."

"Well, I already got that."

"What do you know about Paul Stafford?"

"The piano player? Not a bad piano player . . . well-respected by his fellow musicians. Makes out pretty good for himself with the—" Mr. Clancy paused and looked at my young upturned face. "Well, that is to say, popular with ladies on board."

"Lounge lizard, eh?" I replied, leaning back in my chair and jauntily throwing one arm over its back.

"Yeah. The kind of guy other men want to kick." He grinned.

"You mean he dances too well and has too nice a smile?"

"Yeah, that sort of thing. Anyway, there's something fishy about him. He's got a Canadian passport, but he's got one of those posh English accents. You know, Oxford. He's in a funny racket for a swell. And I've noticed he uses some American slang. Must be occupational. He was born in 1900, that'd make him twenty-seven. Why do you ask? Say, Miss Cooper, he hasn't been annoying you, has he?"

"Of course not," I snapped. Why were men so silly? "It's just that . . . well, that first night on board, he expressed a certain prescience. Said to watch out—oh, it's absurd!" I frowned. I sat forward and restacked my papers unnecessarily.

"Watch out for what?" asked Mr. Clancy eagerly.

"For Twist," I replied. "What can he have meant?"

"If someone had watched out for him," said Jack, "Twist might not be dead."

I was startled. I had imagined Paul Stafford had warned me *against* Twist. But he could also have meant to keep an eye on Twist. Somehow, this interpretation heartened me considerably. I smiled at the thought.

Jack watched my smile, and frowned.

"Hmm," he said.

"What do you know about the professor?" I asked quickly.

"Ignacz Probrislow. Born in Prague, 1881. Some sort of alienist. Specializes in criminal lunacy. But he won't talk. I wanted him to write a little piece for the *Globe*. You know, 'Our Expert on the Scene Investigates Baffling Deck Chair Murder.' But he just mutters, 'It's the work of a madman.' So I told him to write it from that point of view, but no dice. It doesn't figure. He could use the publicity for his upcoming lecture tour. Won't tell me a thing about Twist. Who the hell was Twist anyway, I'd like to know?"

"Other than that he might have been a blackmailer," I replied, "nobody seems to know anything about him."

"Maybe the professor does," said Jack grimly.

CHAPTER SEVEN

I lay in my bunk, hovering in that delicious state between sleep and wakefulness. Above me, the porthole let through a round of clear sunlight. It was going to be a beautiful day. Illuminated dust hovered in the column of light. I thought vaguely about the dust. How strange that there should be dust on the high seas. I wondered sleepily where it had come from, and thought about dust coming from Europe to America in people's clothes and on the soles of their shoes.

Aunt Hermione let a trunk lid descend with a crash. I closed my eyes and feigned sleep, but she had apparently observed a flicker of my eyelids.

"Oh, dear, I really didn't mean to wake you, Iris," she said, slamming down a heavy jar of face cream. "You are awake, aren't you?"

She took my moan for assent.

"Now that you are awake, you must tell me all about your work on the committee. You've been so busy these past two days."

I opened my eyes and smiled. It was hard to be cross with Aunt Hermione. If I confronted her about her thumping around, so obviously designed to wake me, she no doubt would have denied it in all sincerity.

"I've arranged for us to breakfast here in our cabin," she said, "so you can tell me all about the case. In strictest confidence, of course. I'm so eager to hear all."

"I wish there were more to tell," I said, throwing off the covers. I put on my silk kimono and began a search for slippers. "There were only a handful of people on deck, and I'm convinced it has to have been one of them. Anyone else would have been noticed. The motive seems to be blackmail."

"Oh, how delicious," said Aunt Hermione. "That is, of course it's dreadful this Twist fellow was killed, but if you're to have a murder at all, it may as well be an *interesting* one, don't you think so?"

The blond cabin steward, Hawkins, arrived with a breakfast tray, and we fell silent. He deftly arranged toast, boiled eggs, pots of jam and marmalade, and silver tea things, smiled a trifle too broadly, and left. I plunged into my narrative again, telling Aunt Hermione of the blackmail note and of the doctor's medical testimony, listing the suspects, describing Professor Probrislow's strange behavior over the blue ring, and Miss Nadi's lurid past and her fainting spell.

"Really, Iris, I can't imagine why everyone thinks her a great beauty. She has an unhealthy pallor, and she doesn't look well-nourished. In my day, women were supposed to look like women. Why these modern girls want to look like boys I'm sure I don't know. Now, you have a neat little figure, but it's still womanly."

I sighed. Aunt Hermione did not understand why I found my bosom a handicap. "It's the new clothes," I said. "They require a simple, sweeping line." Aunt Hermione clucked. "Why, my friend Harriet wraps her bosom in scarves to flatten it," I continued, "so the clothes look better." I neglected to add that I also indulged in this practice occasionally.

"Dreadful, dreadful." Aunt Hermione shook her head. "But then, when I was a girl, we laced ourselves so very tightly. I'm sure it wasn't healthy. But tell me, dear"—Aunt Hermione placed her teacup neatly in its saucer and leaned over the table—"*whom* do you suspect?"

I leaned back and waved the jam spoon in the air. "I suspect everybody, and I suspect nobody," I said, "or is it the other way around? But mostly I suspect the professor. Nobody really knew Twist, and he really didn't know anybody. The professor says he was a criminal. It's likely he was a blackmailer. In any case, it provides us with a good motive for his murder. And who would he have had ample opportunity to blackmail? His employer. Why, Professor Probrislow said he did his letters and so forth. Suppose he opened a letter addressed to the professor that revealed some scandal? All speculative, of course, but I really don't like the professor at all."

Aunt Hermione was pensive. "Somehow I can't see it. There's something timid about the man. I can't imagine him committing such an overt act."

I thought about the professor's strange story of having engaged Twist with an eye to observing him for scientific purposes. That was a passive act, the act of one of life's observers—not the act of a passionate killer.

"But," continued Aunt Hermione, "there *is* something very odd about the professor. That peculiar soft beard, and those long pale fingers. No, there's something not quite nice about him. And he took Twist's death much too lightly."

"He is strange," I said. "There's a bitterness about him."

"Probably a woman somewhere," said Aunt Hermione.

"Yes, that's what I thought," I replied.

After breakfast, Aunt Hermione joined me in a turn around the deck, and we repaired to the social hall for a mid-morning cup of coffee. While I had been working on the committee, Aunt Hermione, in her usual fashion, had made the acquaintance of a large number of passengers. She greeted many of them gaily and accepted an invitation to join a charming-looking English lady. Mrs. Fitzhugh, engaged in desultory needlework, was a rosy woman with a pert, amusing face. She was, of course, the mother of Bobby and Agnes. She introduced her husband, a good-looking black Irish sort of man, who nodded curtly and continued his perusal of a week-old London newspaper.

"Miss Cooper," said Mrs. Fitzhugh, "your aunt has told us all how you've been locked up in the captain's cabin while they do their sleuthing. How thrilling! Bobby was delighted to be summoned, but poor Agnes was a little unnerved by the experience. I imagine the poor dear has heard all the grisly details from Bobby. He's taken a keen interest in the case."

"It doesn't do to allow them to be frightened," said Aunt Hermione gently. "They tend to nightmares at that age."

"Oh, poor Agnes is always frightened. A very fearful little thing. Bursts into tears at the drop of a hat." Mrs. Fitzhugh shrugged. "But Fräulein Reiter is always nearby."

"Ah, but I always say there's no substitute for a mother's care," said Aunt Hermione, waxing to a favorite theme. "When my sister Julia died, Iris and I took care of the children, Iris's little brothers and sisters. After all, one never knows, really, who these people one *hires* to care for children are."

Mrs. Fitzhugh, blithely unaware that Aunt Hermione spoke for her benefit, readily agreed. "How true. The one before last—well, I'm sorry to say, she drank. But she did mend. Now, the last one wouldn't touch so much as a pillow slip. 'Madame,' she said, 'I do not mend.' "

She continued, "It's not as though they have much else to do. Looking after children can't be that taxing." I contained myself there. "In any case, Fräulein Reiter does mend. And she's very good with the children. Patient and firm. Their German is coming along, too. Edgar's mother felt a German was no longer suitable—the war and all that—but we think a German gives them the discipline they need.

"Fräulein Reiter's been very decent about the wages, too. The wages some of these people want! There's probably something terribly wrong with her, too. We just haven't found it yet. Probably steals teaspoons." Mrs. Fitzhugh laughed gaily.

Captain Fitzhugh looked up from his paper. "Eleanor, that's not fair. I'm sure she didn't take it."

"Good heavens," said Aunt Hermione. "Did you find one missing?"

"Oh, I never said she did," said Mrs. Fitzhugh. "Edgar, I was only joking." She turned to Aunt Hermione. "No, not a teaspoon, a stickpin. Gold thing of Edgar's. It's missing. Really, Edgar, I just thought of her for a moment . . . but that would be foolish. Not really very valuable, was it? I mean, my jewelry or something would make sense. What did happen to it though, Edgar?"

"Oh, it'll turn up," said Edgar absently. "But it won't do to accuse Fräulein Reiter. We were damned lucky to get her. You know we've had trouble with governesses."

The blond cabin steward, Hawkins, loomed up behind Aunt Hermione. He presented me with a silk scarf I'd been wearing on deck.

"Oh, yes," I said. "That is mine. How kind of you."

"No trouble at all, miss," he answered. "I wanted to make sure you got it straightaway. It could blow overboard, a thing like that." He smiled broadly.

"Unctuous fellow," said Captain Fitzhugh when Hawkins had left. "Always have an urge to give him a swift kick."

"Lots of people bring out the kicking instinct in Edgar," said his wife. "And this time, I share it. There really is something unpleasant about that cabin steward. Usually they're such dignified men."

"Oh, here's Mrs. Destinoy-Pinchot," said Aunt Hermione. "I knew her as a girl; she was Gladys Crumm then. Married very well, an Englishman. I noticed her name on the passenger list, and popped down to see her. She's been staying in her cabin, and I tried to get her out and about. Hello, Gladys." Aunt Hermione wheeled a glove in the air. Mrs. Destinoy-Pinchot, a large woman, well-upholstered in stout tweeds, waved gaily back.

She approached us with a tall girl of about my age in tow. I was introduced to Ursula, a hearty-looking young thing with large teeth and a shy manner. Ursula, it appeared, was Mrs.

Destinoy-Pinchot's daughter, on her way to America to meet her American relatives. "I'm so glad, Miss Cooper," said Ursula to Aunt Hermione, "that you convinced mother to come up. It's been frightfully dull." Ursula reddened and twisted a corner of her jacket with large, bony hands.

"Can't abide many people," barked her mother, in what sounded to me like a very English accent. "Glad to have found you, Hermione. So bothersome chaperoning a young girl. Can't wait till Ursula's properly out."

"Things have changed a good deal in America since our day, Gladys," said Aunt Hermione gently. "Why, I let Iris gad about quite on her own. Of course, she's nineteen. Ursula's a little younger. But a girl's best chaperone is herself."

I couldn't imagine Gladys Destinoy-Pinchot ever having been young. Aunt Hermione was quite believable as an ingenue, plump and pink and pretty, with her large, soft eyes, but Mrs. Destinoy-Pinchot seemed always to have been middle-aged.

Ursula regarded me with what I imagined to be envy. I resolved to spend a little time with her; she seemed so awkward and lonely, and probably hadn't been with young people much. But, of course, Ursula would have to come second to my detecting.

The exuberant Mr. Ogle bounded up to us. "Now let's see, you must be the Destinoy-Pinchots. Been lying kind of low, haven't you? You're in the cabin next to mine. Hello, Miss Cooper, Miss Cooper." Ogle nodded to me and my aunt. "Well, I'm glad I've found you. You see, we're getting together an evening's entertainment, and we want everyone to participate. Ship's concert, you know . . ."

Mrs. Destinoy-Pinchot looked aghast. Ursula became very nervous. "You have the advantage of me, sir," said Mrs. Destinoy-Pinchot in deep, gruff tones.

"Ogle, Ogle," he said cheerily. "Sioux Falls. I'm the chairman of the ship's concert. And the mileage pool." He smiled

brightly. "Say, we've got a young people's deck tennis tour-
nament today. Perhaps Miss Destinoy-Pinchot here would
care to participate?"

"She would not," said her mother. "Good day. Come,
Ursula." She wheeled and turned, nodding to us as she left.
"Hermione, do join us for tea later. Shall we see you at
four?"

"Some people just haven't got the proper spirit at all,"
said Mr. Ogle sadly. He bounded away in search of new
quarry.

"Gladys has taken herself much too seriously," said Aunt
Hermione. "They were a good family, but very little money.
Poor Gladys always wore her sisters' old dresses. Proud as
ever, though. A pity she's become so exclusive; it must be
hard on poor Ursula."

We watched the retreating figures of Ursula and her
mother.

"You know, Gladys is simply asking for trouble with that
girl," clucked Aunt Hermione, "sheltering her as she does.
An inexperienced girl like that, and with her fortune, is just
the sort to fall into the clutches of an unscrupulous type of
young man. Remember that horried tango instructor who
ran off with Ida Cartwright's youngest? Reeked of some sort
of perfume, and very oily hair." Aunt Hermione shuddered
at the recollection. "Now you, Iris, are much too sensible to
become entangled with an unsuitable young man."

These musings were interrupted by the arrival of a trio of
older ladies, shipboard acquaintances of Aunt Hermione. I
was introduced, and the ladies beamed at me. "Oh, we've
heard so much about you," they twittered. We sat with them
for a while, and they showed us photographs of their travels.
They were a jolly group, and intrepid tourists who had
braved all sorts of adversity in their quests for enrichment. I
thought to myself how truly plucky older ladies could be, as
I studied snapshots of these three mounted on camels, standing against rugged crags in alpinists' gear, and struggling

with a punt on the Thames, and I was proud of my country-women. Older European ladies we had met were inevitably soberly clad in dark clothes and were unaccustomed to fending for themselves, and no doubt would have been terrified at the prospect of traveling unescorted in foreign lands. Presently, the ladies swept Aunt Hermione away to the bridge table. I assured my aunt that I could amuse myself, and began to wander idly through the ship's public rooms.

I paused outside the dining saloon when I heard the strains of the piano coming from within. I had planned to tell the committee about the odd warnings I'd received from Paul Stafford. But I hadn't. Something had stopped me. Now I decided to pursue the matter myself.

I entered the dining saloon, where white-clad waiters swarmed, brushing breakfast crumbs off the tables in a practiced manner, flourishing napery and silver, and arranging single roses in the crystal vases on the tables in preparation for lunch. The soft strains of the piano came from behind the potted palms.

Paul Stafford sat at his piano, a pencil between his teeth. He appeared to be composing. The tune he played was a jazz tune with a jazz rhythm, but the chords were haunting, with the sob of a gypsy's violin.

"What do you want?" He scowled.

I sat next to him on the piano bench. He continued to play. "Why did you tell me to watch out for Mr. Twist?" I asked softly. The strange, haunting melody continued.

"Did I say that?" he asked dreamily over the melody.

"Of course you did. You know you did. Whatever did you mean?"

"I warned you. It was foolish of me, but, well, I warned you. And I can't tell you any more about it."

"Are you going to tell the committee what you know?"

"No. I have my reasons."

"Well, then, I must tell them."

"If you do, you will only make things worse," he replied.

"Look," I said amiably, "the professor seems to think Twist was some kind of a crook. Is that what you meant? To watch out for him because he was a crook? Or did you mean to watch out for him in the other sense? To look out for him?"

My only answer was another snatch of melody.

"If you know something, you should tell the committee," I said. "After all, it will make you look suspicious if you don't." I was sorry as soon as I added that last. I realized I didn't want Paul Stafford to look suspicious. To me, or to the committee. But mostly to me.

Paul Stafford stopped playing and glared at me. Suddenly I was frightened. He seemed to see the fear in my eyes, for his face took on a look of triumph.

"Perhaps you think I am the killer," he said. "Perhaps it is better that you think that. Then I can frighten you into silence." He grabbed me by my shoulders. "Do not betray me. My warning was very real. And so is the one I give you now. *Do not betray me.*"

My fear turned to anger. "I am not afraid," I said.

He released me and pounded out a strong, angry, dissonant chord. The quiet clink of the china and silver stopped for a moment. He turned to me.

"I will do what must be done," he said. "I swear this on my honor, which is no small thing. There are forces at work which you cannot understand."

I rose, shaking with anger, and left him. The waiters watched me curiously as I passed through the dining saloon.

I stood at the rail of the promenade deck, trying to understand the strong feelings Paul Stafford invoked in me after every one of our obscure and volatile conversations. Why was he so angry? And what was his secret?

"Do you know how to make a boat?" inquired a small voice.

I smiled down at little Bobby Fitzhugh. He handed me a square of paper, and I folded it neatly into the shape of a boat.

"Here you are," I said.

"Oh, thank you. Fräulein doesn't know how to make boats."

"Well, I'm sure she knows how to do all sorts of other things."

"Yes, Mummy says she's very intelligent. Speaks all sorts of languages. We have her so we can learn to speak German. Can you speak German? My sister and I can. We can count and we understand everything she says. But she doesn't know how to make boats." He paused for breath before launching once more into his narrative. "And she's always fussing. She tucks everyone in and ties their shoes and carries on. I think it's silly. She has letters from abroad sometimes, though, and that's nice. For the stamps, you know. Our last governess just had a sister in Scotland. I collect stamps. I've got stamps with birds on them and with kings and some with flowers, and I soak them off the envelopes, and for my birthday I'm getting a book to put them in. My sister doesn't collect stamps. She's too little, she's only six. I'm eight. On my birthday I'll be nine. Would you like to see some of my stamps?"

"Oh, dear, Bobby, we mustn't annoy the lady." Fräulein Reiter joined us.

"I like to talk to Bobby," I said.

"She made me a boat. Look," said Bobby.

"Fräulein, fräulein, it's gone wrong again," said the little girl at Fräulein Reiter's side, handing up a dirty-looking square of pink knitting. "The loops are getting so tight. I think I may cry."

"Oh, I don't think you will," said the governess, examining the pink square. "You mustn't pull at it so. Let's see. We'll just go backward, so, and then you can begin again. Remember now, wrap the wool around the needle with your hand. Here is the difficult part, but you can do it. Say it to yourself. Through, between, down, lift."

I gazed with sympathy at Agnes. I remembered my first efforts, all twisted and full of knots. And Miss Laurence hadn't been as patient. She'd seize my knitting, wrap the yarn herself, and thrust it back at me. She'd punctuated "through, between, down, and lift" with scolding and slaps.

"Now come, children, we shall have a nice tea very soon, so we must wash carefully. Come with me."

"I'm perfectly clean," said Bobby indignantly, but he and Agnes were shepherded away. I noticed a smudgy envelope at my feet. I opened it, and a shower of stamps fell out. Bobby's collection, I imagined. I stopped to pick them up, and I'd gathered most of them together when Jack Clancy came by.

"Say, I'm disappointed. You don't collect stamps, do you? Always thought it was a pretty stupid thing to do," he said amiably. "Coins just as stupid. Can I help?"

"A little boy left these here," I explained. "I think I've got them all."

He bent and extricated another stamp from beneath my foot. "Here's the last one."

I took it and was startled. It was a smudgy blue stamp with the word "Graznia." It bore the portrait in profile of a man—a profile that looked oddly familiar. In fact, it was because I'd seen Paul Stafford first in profile, at his piano, that I recognized him. It looked like the same face, all right: the chiseled features, the well-shaped forehead, and chin were the same.

Jack Clancy didn't seem to notice my reaction. I composed myself. There was no sense getting the volatile reporter on a rampage, if I wasn't absolutely sure. And besides, in some odd way I felt a loyalty to Paul Stafford. Or was it fear?

I slipped it into my pocket and Mr. Clancy didn't notice I

hadn't put it with the others. "How about it, Miss Cooper?" he asked. "Now that the committee's all finished up, maybe you and I should team up like we talked about before. Become detectives. We both know the committee isn't any closer to a solution than we are. Tell me your views of the case." He leaned back and assumed a serious expression.

"Really, Mr. Clancy, I know very little about the whole business, and your attempts to extract information from me are most transparent."

"Doesn't seem to make much difference," said Jack. "I find people like to tell me things just as much when I come right out and pump 'em as when I'm not so transparent. I'm the straightforward type. I'm not ashamed of my calling. It's my job to get people to tell me things. I'm pretty good at it, too. But I admit when I've met my match, Miss Cooper." He smiled disarmingly. "You're a tough nut to crack, yessir.

"Say, I wish I knew more about this ring business. Seems that's what sent the Nadi dame to the mat. What'd it look like again?"

"We've been over this." I sighed. "You saw the ring yourself when Hawkins brought it in."

"Looked pretty ordinary to me," he said. "Aw, hell. Vera Nadi'll use any excuse for a little cheap drama."

"You seem to be one of the few men on board immune to her charms," I said, turning from him and gazing out over the rail.

"I like 'em a little fresher. You know, this case has got me beat. I'm getting mean wires from my editor. He wants some hot copy on this thing, and I can't give it to him. It's plain discouraging."

He sounded so genuinely forlorn and comical that I laughed out loud. "I think you work too hard," I said.

"Yeah, you're probably right. All work and no play. Trouble is, I've been working all my life. Started as a copyboy for the paper at twelve. Before that, I sold the *Globe* on street corners. I loved it; it was a swell way to grow up.

Plenty of excitement. We had a lot of extras in those days."
Mr. Clancy looked happily nostalgic. "But you're probably
right. I guess I do work too hard."

I thought of Jack Clancy when Aunt Hermione and I
presented ourselves at Mrs. Destinoy-Pinchot's cabin for tea
later that afternoon. "Aunt Hermione," I whispered, "do let
me spirit poor Ursula away."

"Good idea, Iris. You're a kind girl." Aunt Hermione
patted my hand and a maid admitted us to their cabin. It was
the best one on the ship, and included a small, charming sitting room—which was a good thing, for otherwise the
Destinoy-Pinchots' habit of exclusivity would have required
them to spend the day weaving among their trunks and sitting on their beds.

After a decent interval, I suggested that Ursula and I go on
deck and get some air. "Good idea," said Aunt Hermione.
"Gladys and I can talk over our girlhood adventures; you
young people wouldn't be interested, I'm sure."

"Don't loll about the public rooms," said Ursula's mother
as we left.

I was correct in guessing I'd find Mr. Clancy at the bar.
Ursula looked nervous as I approached him; I'm sure she
thought I was going to sit at the bar and toss off a half bottle
of gin.

"All work and no play, eh?" I said archly. "I see you've
found a way to relax."

"I'm really not much of a drinker," said Mr. Clancy. "I've
been pumping the smoking room steward here. I figure
maybe the murderer's been drinking away his guilt. People
tell bartenders everything, you know."

"Well, why don't you join me and Miss Destinoy-Pinchot
here in some wholesome deck games?"

Jack Clancy winced.

"Oh, I know they're kind of silly, but I think a little
mindless amusement will do you good. Ursula, this is Jack
Clancy."

"Pleased to meet you," said Mr. Clancy. "Anyway, I don't know how to play any of these deck games."

"Not even shuffleboard?"

"Nope."

"Neither do I," said Ursula.

Mr. Ogle, who had been going over the books of the daily mileage pool with the smoking room steward, had obviously overheard us.

"What?" he exclaimed, rushing to my side. "Don't know how to play shuffleboard? Ridiculous. Come with me. I'm just about to begin the ship decathlon up on the promenade deck. Oh, we've got a grand program. Gunnysack races, the old egg and spoon, and some swell new ones. Passing an orange from person to person without using your hands. It's a real corker. And we're having a contest where the ladies have to light a cigarette in the gentlemen's mouths, and we give 'em one match and they don't get to strike it on the box or on the deck."

"What do they do, bite it?" asked Jack.

"Oh, they're ingenious. They manage to get them lit, but it's a struggle. And terrific good fun."

Poor Ursula looked as if she thought Mr. Ogle's program did indeed sound like fun. She had developed two enthusiastic bright red spots in her cheeks. "Oh, let's do join in," she said eagerly.

"Golly," muttered Jack, "If that's relaxing, I think I'd rather work." But he tossed off his drink and accompanied us to the promenade deck.

Mr. Ogle, wearing, for some reason, a whistle on a cord around his neck, took immediate charge of the proceedings. Occasionally he blew the whistle, but I could discern no pattern in his blowing, and assumed he was simply expressing his abundant enthusiasm. He put a gathering of passengers through their ridiculous paces, and although Jack muttered "tomfoolery" and questioned the fairness of the rules Mr. Ogle had made up, he seemed to be having a good time.

Poor Ursula was quite giddy with happiness, and jumped
up and down with such zeal after winning some sort of contest involving an India rubber ball attached to a mashie-
niblick, that Mr. Ogle had great difficulty pinning her winning badge onto her tweed bosom.

Jack's enthusiasm increased when he had arranged for
some small side bets on the outcome of the contests, and after he had won a three-legged race by dint of having dragged
his partner, a small man tied firmly to his leg, across the
finish line.

"Mr. Ogle is such a fascinating man," said Ursula. "How
kind of him to organize these games and see that everyone is
having such fun. Who is he, actually? I mean . . ."

Ursula, I imagined, like most Europeans, was having
problems in distinguishing the class of Americans she met.
Ursula's American-born mother had certainly raised her as
the complete Englishwoman.

"Millionaire from Sioux Falls," said Jack. "Puts in twenty-
hour days making sure no one gets any rest. But I must admit, girls, I've enjoyed myself. And I'm ten bucks to the good
betting on these ridiculous contests. I wish I could do as well
with the ponies. What do you say we have ourselves a couple
of cocktails on the proceeds?" Jack gave us each an arm, but
Ursula protested regretfully that she must get back to her
cabin.

I accompanied her, and we discovered Aunt Hermione and
her girlhood friend convulsed in delightful giggles. Ursula
seemed surprised to see her mother in such good spirits.

Later, Aunt Hermione told me that she had broken
through her old friend's reserve. "Still the same giddy
Gladys underneath it all. I think this trip to America will do
her good. And the girl, too. I think poor Gladys has been
trying so hard to fit into English society that she's out-
Englished them. Whey, she told me she rides to the hounds
sidesaddle! Can you imagine?"

I certainly could. "Ursula and I had a very jolly time, too,"

I said. "She was making a perfect idiot of herself and enjoying it thoroughly."

Back at our cabin, we were surprised to discover Mr. Clancy, bearing a lovely spray of white orchids. "Had to spend my winnings in some frivolous fashion. Here you are, Iris. Thanks for helping me take my mind off my work."

Aunt Hermione looked inquisitive. "Mr. Clancy joined us for deck games," I explained. "Oh, they're lovely, you shouldn't have."

"Why not?" asked Jack. "I never met a girl that didn't like orchids. So long." And he marched down the corridor, whistling.

They were lovely; creamy, waxy, delicate things. As we dressed for dinner, Aunt Hermione fixed one in my hair. "There, it stands out beautifully against the gold. Really, they are dreadfully expensive. Perhaps I shouldn't have allowed you to receive them." She looked dubious.

I studied my reflection. I did look very nice, I thought with satisfaction. I wore a creamy pale gown with the slightest hint of peach, and, with the peach tones in my skin and the red-gold in my hair, I looked very rosy and glowing. I had turned out much better than anyone, especially me, had expected. My childhood freckles had faded, and my long hazel eyes, a queer mixture of gold and green that I'd always hated, looked sparkling and intelligent and lively. I decided then and there that I really didn't want round, dewy, cornflower blue ones after all.

After I had dressed, I sat down and looked again at Bobby's Graznian stamp. "Take a look at this, Aunt Hermione. Does this look familiar to you?"

Aunt Hermione had been applying two little circles of rouge. "Hmm? Let me see?" She peered at it intently for a second or two. "Well, it's a postage stamp," she said, puzzled.

"You don't think the person on it looks familiar?"

"Well, sort of. Mostly it just looks marbly and white. But

then everyone on a postage stamp looks rather the same, don't they? Why do you ask?" She began rubbing the circles of rouge, feathering out the edges.

"I thought it looked a little like the piano player on this ship."

"Well, I can't see what he would be doing on a postage stamp. Iris, you're beinning to sound rather fanciful, dear. I hope you haven't developed a tendresse for the piano player. That would account for your seeing his face on a postage stamp when it really wasn't."

"I suppose it would," I answered, still staring at the stamp. Finally I put it in the locket I always wear around my neck—an oval-shaped locket on a long chain, with a picture of my mother in it.

When we arrived at our table in the dining saloon, Mrs. Griffin was leaning across the table, interrogating the professor.

CHAPTER EIGHT

"**I** think it's mighty peculiar, that's what I think," she said, eyeing Probrislow with obvious suspicion. "You knew that this Twist character was a criminal and you went ahead and hired him?"

"Please," said the professor wearily. "Let us not discuss this unfortunate incident any more. My nerves, they are not able to stand up to this punishment. It is most trying."

"I can believe that," said Mrs. Griffin.

"I wish they'd take away Mr. Twist's chair," said Aunt Hermione. It *was* unsettling. We all stared at the chair. I half-expected to see Mr. Twist appear in it, smiling his smile full of crooked teeth.

The professor looked at the chair and shuddered. We all shifted our gaze to him: the colonel, Aunt Hermione and I, the judge and Mrs. Griffin. Small drops of sweat began to appear on Probrislow's forehead. He mopped at his brow with a handkerchief.

The waiter arrived, and Aunt Hermione attempted to break the awkwardness with exclamations over the food. "Such a fine glaze on those carrots," she exclaimed. "Really, the cuisine on this ship is excellent. Not at all what they say English food can be like."

"Nothing wrong with English food," barked the colonel. "It's good wholesome fare, and properly cooked. Can't abide these continental vegetables just passed through a bit of steam. You need to boil properly to get the germs out. Filthy germs and microbes, they need to be properly boiled away. Can't tell that to the French. God knows what muck lurks in a French meal. Give me a properly cooked, wholesome English meal any time. Not that I don't mind a decently turned out curry once in a while."

While the colonel had carried on this somewhat unpleasant discourse, the waiter slipped a small, folded note under the edge of my plate.

I took it, managed to open it with one hand, and read it in my lap.

I've been a boor. I must explain myself. Meet me at the first lifeboat station when the orchestra breaks at ten.
Paul Stafford.

I gasped. What could this mean? I was frightened, but determined to meet him. He could have a clue to the mystery, and I had to find out all I could.

At ten, I walked out onto the boat deck. For a crazy moment, I wondered if I'd be pitched overboard into the dark water below. But I had to find out what I could.

"Iris," he called out. I strode toward the shadowy figure by the rail. It was misty and I could barely make out his form.

"You'll be cold," he said, and slipped his jacket over my shoulders. "Iris, I had to see you. I feel I've been abominable. I've been thinking it over, and . . . I didn't mean to frighten you. I mean, well, actually I did, but I'm sorry now. I can't tell you everything. But I want you to know I am not a murderer. You have my word of honor. I tried to make you think that, so you wouldn't put yourself in danger. But somehow I couldn't stand for you to think that of me."

"You must explain yourself," I said. "You can't give me these peculiar warnings and menacing advice about not interfering without explaining yourself. I want to know why you warned me about Twist. I want to know why you said you hate the professor. What do you know about this business?

"That first evening, when we danced, you called Twist a

rabbity little fellow, and you laughed at him. Well, it doesn't matter who he was, whether he was a crook or a blackmailer or just a simple young man sailing away on his first adventure, he shouldn't have been cut down like that. Nobody has the right to do that to anybody, and if you know something about it, you should speak up."

He gazed at me from beneath dark lashes. "I wish I knew what I should do," he said softly. "Believe me, I want to do the right thing. That is a wonderful speech you just made. You have a natural sense of honor, and of what is right."

"Of course I do," I said. "Everyone does. Or should."

"I wish it were simpler," he replied.

I touched the locket with the stamp in it and wondered if I should ask him about the portrait.

"Don't get all obscure again," I snapped. "I can't bear it. Why can't you be more direct?"

He took me in his arms and kissed me. I kissed him back. As we clung together, the mist parted to reveal the moon for a moment.

"This doesn't make any sense at all," I murmured.

"Of course not," he replied. "It never does." He smiled down at me and traced my cheekbone with his hand. "Iris, you are magnificent," he said, and fastened the orchid in my hair, which had come loose. I stood very still and explored his face with my eyes.

"Perhaps," he said, "You will give me the courage to do what is right. But I don't know yet just how." He took my hand and kissed it. "And when I do, Iris, I will come to you and tell you everything."

We heard the strains of the orchestra tuning up. I slipped out of Paul's jacket and watched him walk back through the mist.

I wasn't sure just what I thought. I knew only that I was no longer afraid of Paul Stafford. But should I have been? He was a very troubled young man.

• • •

The next couple of days passed slowly. I learned nothing more about the murder, and I felt as if my curiosity had begun to burn itself out. I grew restless, and chalked it up to the confinement of shipboard life. The *Irenia* was a small ship, built before the war, and was certainly no Blue Riband competitor. Aunt Hermione had chosen her for her slowness. She was convinced that speed was a danger and made collision with icebergs more probable, and she relished the idea of a long time aboard ship to recuperate from the rigors of travel. Now it seemed to me as if we had seen nothing but ocean for months.

"Iris, you look peaky," said Aunt Hermione. "You're not in love or anything, are you?" She eyed the orchids on the dresser with new interest.

"No, no. I'm just fine. There's nothing wrong with me at all," I lied. I let Aunt Hermione organize a complicated program of bridge and sitting in deck chairs with her shipboard acquaintances, a lively group of American widows and spinsters returning from foreign travel. Jack Clancy taught me to play gin rummy, which we did in companionable silence for great stretches of time, and I returned the envelope with the rest of Bobby's stamps. I read a silly, girlish novel about a madcap duchess who fell in love with a sultan, and I wondered about Paul Stafford. The strange tune he'd been composing began to haunt me. I wondered if he would be able to decide upon an honorable course of action, and let me in on his secret.

After two days of this restlessness, I threw down my book, which I'd been reading in desultory fashion, and set out for a nighttime stroll. The night air would cure me of my restlessness. I muffled myself in a greatcoat and headed for the promenade deck. I took one turn, felt cold and lonely, and settled in my deck chair and looked at the stars etched against the darkening sky. A lavender cloud drifted across a pale crescent moon.

Presently, I heard voices. I thought of clearing my throat

to let whoever was there know I could hear them, but I decided instead to sit very still. Two shadowly figures stood together at the rail. Two cigarettes glowed in the dusk.

"I truly loved him. It was an affair of the heart. I tell you, my friend, the worst day of my life was when that odious Rasneski appeared to ruin our happiness forever." The voice was unmistakable, the rich contralto voice of Vera Nadi.

"When I saw the ring the other day, it all came flooding back. I could smell the bougainvillea that grew outside our hotel room in Nice, I could feel the sea breeze, and I could feel the pain once more. And just as these memories came flooding back into my soul, I recognized him. Baron Rasneski." The voice caught in a slight croak. Vera Nadi was crying.

"I had only seen him once before, all those years ago, and then our interview lasted but half an hour. But it was the most tragic half hour of my life."

I sat up in my chair, straining to catch every word. To whom was Miss Nadi speaking?

But Aunt Hermione came to my side, and her voice startled the shadowy figures at the rail. "Iris! Is that you?" They moved farther into the dark.

"Iris? Are you there? It's rather chilly, isn't it, dear?"

I followed my aunt inside, sure that Vera Nadi had been discussing her royal romance. But with whom? I did know one thing. Vera Nadi had truly loved the man she spoke of.

The ring must have been the royal seal the judge had mentioned. Or at least something to do with the royal house of Graznia. And this Baron Rasneski, he had something to do with the royal house, too, or at least with the royal scandal. And he was on board. Who could he be? Only the professor. Rasneski sounded like a Slavic name, and Vera Nadi saw the ring for the only time when the professor had sat across from her. And he had insisted it was his. Could the Comrades of the New Dawn be involved? The colonel had said they were meddling in the politics of Graznia.

The pieces began to fit. I resolved to discuss what I now knew with the colonel. But what did I know? Perhaps the colonel, who seemed up on Graznian politics, would have more pieces to the puzzle.

"Aunt Hermione," I said breathlessly, "I must see the colonel. I think I have discovered something about this business." I kissed her and rushed off, leaving her bewildered. The colonel, I imagined, could be found in the smoking room.

He was there, in front of a fire, sitting in a large armchair, nursing a brandy and soda, staring morosely into the flames. "Hello Colonel Marris," I said. "I wonder if you could spare a moment or two."

He looked up at me rather blearily. His face was ruddy. His eyes were glazed. There was little doubt in my mind that the colonel was rather worse for drink. That was fine with me. If brandy had loosened his tongue it would suit my purpose.

"I understand you're up on Graznian affairs," I said, settling into the club chair opposite his.

"Want a spot of something?" he said vaguely. "A sherry or something?"

"No thank you." I leaned forward. "What would you say if I told you Baron Rasneski was aboard. You know who he is, don't you?"

"Hmm? Rasneski on board. That's right. But there's no need for you to know about that. Dangerous stuff, young lady. Shouldn't be mixing in. Seem like a nice, plucky girl. Mustn't get hurt." His eyes turned on me with an intensity that surprised me. "How on earth did you spot him?"

"Could this Rasneski have something to do with the Comrades of the New Dawn?" I hazarded.

"What? Not likely. Although the old schemer is probably capable of anything. Know something about his going over to the other side?"

"Not really," I said airily. I really didn't know a thing, but by letting the colonel think I did I seemed to be getting something out of him. Actually, it seemed likely that Rasneski had something to do with the royal house of Graznia, from the way Vera Nadi had talked.

"Well, if you know Rasneski's position as adviser to the royal house, you know that his aims and the aims of the Comrades are at odds. He's the one that kept the hopes of a return of the Graznian monarchy alive. I guess those hopes are gone now." His eyes seemed to be filled with tears. "Dash it all, how can you fight these fanatics when they won't come out and fight like men?"

I was pretty sure that Rasneski was Professor Probrislow from what I'd overheard Vera Nadi say, but I wanted to make sure. "Interesting, his choosing to pose as a criminologist," I said. 'Has he any real experience along those lines?"

"None. A very unconvincing pose, I thought. All that nonsense about Lombroso. Ridiculous. Part of the little comedy he chose to play with the person he called Twist, I imagine. If anyone asked too many questions about his secretary he could come up with this ridiculous story about studying criminal behavior. Rasneski's a pretty thorough fellow."

He took a sip of his drink and said: "But you must tell me how you spotted him. What do you know about Rasneski? He's kept out of the public eye for years."

Rather apologetically, because the colonel would learn that he had told me more than he had to, I told him what I had overheard at the ship's rail.

"And you had no idea to whom the actress was speaking?"

"No."

"Foolish woman. I imagine it was Rasneski who was sent to try to buy her off when she ran off with King Nicholas, and she met him then. I wish I knew to whom she was speaking."

"Colonel Marris," I said. "Who was Twist?"

He laughed bitterly. "Twist? Twist was the thing that's kept Rasneski going all these years. But he failed. And, God help me, so have I." He put a hand out for his glass, then pushed it away. He looked at me sharply. "We mustn't talk about this anymore. It's dangerous. Run along now, and keep out of this business. Telling anyone what you've told me could be dangerous. And I'll speak to your aunt and tell her you're meddling in something dangerous if you don't stop.

"I've said too much, Miss Cooper. Don't you make the same mistake. And *don't* discuss any of this with that reporter friend of yours if you know what's good for you. He could be dangerous himself."

Aunt Hermione was asleep when I returned to our cabin. I was glad, as I hadn't the energy to discuss my recent revelations with her. I undressed quietly and lay in the dark, listening to the steady throb of the *Irenia*'s diesel engines. I knew more than I had ever dared hope, but I still despaired over solving the mystery that was Paul Stafford. At last I slept, but I slept fitfully.

CHAPTER NINE

I really was nervous about the colonel telling my aunt I was in danger. Of course, I didn't believe I was in any danger at all. It was clear to me that the colonel had wanted to solve the case himself and had failed, and didn't want anyone else to have the satisfaction. But I knew that Aunt Hermione would be alarmed if he spoke to her. She was always concerned that she wasn't a good chaperone, and there was no need to worry her unduly. I vowed to steer clear of Colonel Marris and pursue things on my own.

The next morning I sat on deck, wrapped in a large lap robe, an unread book propped up in front of me. Aunt Hermione had gone off to play bridge and I was planning my next move.

"Thought I'd never catch you alone," said Jack Clancy, standing before me with a smile, holding his hat in his hand. "I wanted to talk to you."

The colonel's warning came briefly to mind, but I repressed the thought. Jack Clancy shared my enthusiasm for detecting. "About the case?" I said. He nodded. "Won't you sit down?" I said, indicating Aunt Hermione's deck chair.

"Just had an interesting little talk with Bobby Fitzhugh," Jack said. "He's quite a pal of mine. He tells me you forgot to return one of those stamps he dropped."

"Did I?" I frowned. "And you volunteered to fetch it?"

"Frankly, it wouldn't have interested me in the least if he hadn't told me it was a stamp from Graznia. It's weird. A fellow can go through life never hearing about Graznia. And suddenly it pops up all the time."

Jack Clancy was an observant fellow. I wondered whether he would see a likeness between the portrait on the stamp and Paul Stafford.

"Wait here," I said. "I'll get it and you can give it back to him. I remember now. It was caught in the lining of my pocket and I left it in my cabin," I lied to Jack, and to my surprise found how easy it was. I didn't want to make a big fuss about the stamp because he might come to the same conclusion Aunt Hermione did—that I was smitten with Paul Stafford and saw his face everywhere. That's why I didn't want him to know I was carrying the thing around in my locket, either. I went all the way back to our cabin, took the stamp out of its hiding place around my neck, and brought it back to our deck chairs.

When I returned, Jack Clancy was stretched out on Aunt Hermione's deck chair fast asleep. He looked especially young when he was asleep. I realized then that, despite his brash, worldly manner, he was probably not much older than I. He looked sweet, lying there, with his curly eyelashes resting on his cheeks and his mouth settled into a half smile.

I patted him on the shoulder and his gray-green eyes flew open. "Hello, Iris," he said in a sleepy voice. I felt a strange intimacy as I bent over him and looked into his face.

An instant later, the moment had passed, and I was arranging my own lap robe around me while Jack examined the stamp. "Remind you of anyone?" I asked.

"You bet it does," he replied. "This character here is a dead ringer for that smooth piano player. And, Iris, notice anything else?" He handed me the stamp. "Look behind the portrait."

I did. Very faintly, in smudgy dots, was the shape of a peacock, its feathers fanned out. "Seen that motif before?" asked Jack.

"The ring! The ring had a peacock carved on the back of the stone. I saw it. But how did you see it?"

Jack shrugged. "I had that steward, Hawkins, give me a

good look at the thing before he took it to the room where you and the committee were. Wonder if this means the blue ring is some sort of royal dingus."

"Why, that would make all kinds of sense," I exclaimed. I was so excited I decided to throw caution to the wind and forget what Colonel Marris had told me. Jack Clancy had a keen mind and could help me untangle the mystery. Briefly, I outlined the conversation I'd overheard at the ship's rail.

"Now we're getting somewhere," said Jack. "You know, it may be time to have a little talk with that colonel fellow. He seems up on this Graznian business. Remember, he told us all about it before."

"I already talked to the colonel," I said. "And I don't think he'll tell you a thing. He doesn't want to talk about it." The last thing I wanted was for Jack to rush in and let the colonel know I'd done exactly the opposite of what he'd told me, namely, telling Jack Clancy what I'd overheard. Neither did I want the colonel to get all fired up and have that little chat with Aunt Hermione.

"Won't talk, eh?" said Jack purposefully. "We'll see about that."

"Please don't," I said. "I practically promised him I wouldn't tell anyone, and if he learns I did . . . ."

"Then he won't tell you anything more," said Jack.

"That's right. Besides, he kept telling me not to mix into this business, and," I continued, rather embarrassed, "he said he'd tell Aunt Hermione I was in danger if I kept poking around trying to solve the case."

"Can't have that," said Jack.

"It's not," I said with dignity, "that I'm afraid Aunt Hermione will *forbid* me to pursue this. After all, I'm practically grown up. It's just that I don't want her unduly alarmed."

"Of course, of course," said Jack, patting my hand. "Well, we'll have to take another tack. Tell me, though, what you did get out of the old bird?"

"Well," I said, incredibly relieved that Jack wouldn't

betray me to Colonel Marris, "I went in and asked him about this Rasneski that I'd overheard Vera Nadi talking about, and who had to be Professor Probrislow. But I don't think he would have told me a thing if he hadn't had a little too much brandy and soda. The brandy I mean, not the soda," I added, realizing I was beginning to sound like Aunt Hermione.

"Go on," said Jack impatiently.

"He told me that Rasneski was an adviser to the royal house of Graznia, someone who'd schemed for years to get the monarchy restored."

"Which is just what those Comrades of the New Dawn don't want," said Jack. "The colonel said they wanted to grab the place and turn it into an anarchist's paradise."

"Anyway," I went on, "he said Professor Probrislow wasn't a criminologist at all, and that it was all an elaborate ruse to drag Mr. Twist around and pretend he was a criminal in case anyone got curious.

"And you know," I concluded, "the interesting thing is that Colonel Marris seemed to take all this so personally. He said, 'I failed,' as if it were somehow his fault that Twist was killed. And he said that Rasneski failed, too."

"Failed at getting his boy back on the throne, I guess," said Jack.

An idea began to form in my mind. "Or maybe—Jack, what did Professor Probrislow really need a secretary for anyway if he isn't really Professor Probrislow?"

"If he's Baron Rasneski, throneside schemer," replied Jack, "all he'd really need is—"

"A prince," we said simultaneously.

"That's what the colonel meant," I said, "when he talked about Rasneski's having Twist to keep him going all these years. And it explains why Twist had that ring with the seal of Graznia on it. And it explains why he was killed. Mr. Twist was the prince, traveling incognito with his adviser to escape the assassins of the Comrades of the New Dawn."

"What a story," said Jack under his breath. "What a

story." He grabbed my arm. "Didn't you find out who Vera Nadi was talking to that night?"

"Well, no. I didn't want to pry."

"Swell," said Jack sarcastically. "Don't you want to find out more about this?"

"Well, of course I do," I said. "Now we have to find out who could be an agent for these Comrades of the New Dawn."

"There's still something missing," mused Jack. "If Twist was the prince, traveling incognito, why is the professor sticking to that story about his being a criminal? Why is he keeping mum about the whole thing?"

"Who knows," I said. "He's probably working up some new scheme to restore the monarchy. With someone else. I mean, maybe Mr. Twist had a brother or something who'd succeed. Maybe the professor doesn't want a big investigation right now, while he's in the middle of his schemes. There's so much we don't know."

We sat in silence for a while. My brain reeled with all the new information I had and all the theories we had bandied about.

Presently, I said, "So this blackmail business has all been a blind."

"We have only Vera Nadi's word that there was a blackmailer on board. And she never produced the note."

"But the professor had this story about Twists's having been a blackmailer."

"Yes," said Jack. "But he probably came up with that to fit Miss Nadi's story."

"It's true," I replied. "In the committee meeting he kind of hedged around before he came up with that story." I turned to Jack. "You told me you'd heard something about that before I told you. Where did you hear it?"

Jack smiled. "Confidential source. Not the professor. But all I heard was that Twist was a jailbird."

"But he wasn't. He was a prince." I thought for a moment.

"You know, Jack, Mr. Twist didn't seem like a prince at all. He was a terrible dancer."

"What does that prove? I'm a terrific dancer and I can assure you I'm not a prince."

"He didn't look like a prince at all," I said emphatically.

"And I guess I know who you think should be a prince, if looks and suave manners mean anything," said Jack. He handed back the Graznian postage stamp he'd been holding.

I took it and put it back in my locket.

"Carrying it next to your heart?" he said, with a trace of malice.

"It might be an important clue," I said.

"Well, if you think he's a prince, why don't you ask him about it?" said Jack. "If you don't, I will."

I didn't want to ask Paul Stafford if he was a prince. I wanted him to confide in me of his own volition, just as he'd promised he would, as soon as he sorted out in his mind whatever it was that seemed to be troubling him. I remembered that kiss in the moonlight. Rushing in with a lot of questions might put him off. And, besides, if Paul knew I thought he was a prince, he might think I was one of those silly, royalty-mad American girls like Marjorie Klepp, the cotter-pin heiress.

"Listen, Iris. Forget about the prince. Let's take a look at what we've learned. All this Graznian stuff is based on what we've learned from Colonel Marris. I think we need to find out where he fits in all this."

"Well, you promised we wouldn't talk to him," I said. "He'll make a fuss with Aunt Hermione."

"We don't need to talk to him. I'll just keep an eye on him."

"All right," I said, relieved Jack had abandoned discussing Paul Stafford.

My relief was short-lived.

"By the way, Iris, you do realize, don't you, that if Paul Stafford is a prince he probably knows exactly why Twist was killed. That Twist was killed in his place?"

The moral significance of this eluded me just then. Instead, my first thought was that Paul Stafford was in danger. "There might be a second murder," I said. "He should be warned."

"That's a good excuse to find out who the fellow really is," said Jack.

"Oh, please don't talk to him just yet," I pleaded.

"Why not? Do you know what a big story this is?"

"We've got three days before Montreal. And the captain won't let you wire your paper anyway. Give me a day or so. *I'll* talk to Paul Stafford." Silently I hoped that Paul would confide in me. He'd said he would when the time was right. Perhaps I'd have to hasten the time.

"I can't promise that," said Jack peevishly.

"Oh, please," I said, putting a hand on his jacket sleeve and staring up at him. He really had a rather kind face.

"Come on, Iris, don't look at me like that," he said, averting his eyes.

"Please," I repeated softly.

"Oh, all right. You've got twenty-four hours to get him to come clean." With a frown he rose, clamped on his hat, and marched away.

I thought I knew where I'd find Paul, and I was right. He was in the dining saloon, approaching the piano. The room was empty.

"May we talk?" I said nervously.

He turned. "Iris," he said. It was a simple statement of fact, but the way he said it sent shivers through me. I closed my eyes for a moment and told the shivers to go away.

"Last night," I said, "you promised me you'd tell me your deep, dark secrets. Are you ready?"

"No. I'm not." He stroked my cheek. "I'm going to play and think. When nothing else in the world makes sense, my music does."

"Paul, I know about Rasneski. I know about Twist. At least I think I do. And I think I know who you are."

. His face grew pale and his blue eyes widened. "No," he said. "Don't say another word."

He glanced around nervously. We were completely alone.

I decided to show him the postage stamp and see what his reaction would be. I reached into my jacket, fishing for the chain of my locket.

"No," he said. "Not you. It can't be." He stepped backward, staring at me with a look of genuine horror.

I froze, my hand still poised over the locket chain. "What is it?" I said, and then, with a great shock, I knew. He was staring now at my hand reaching inside my jacket. I let it drop and he seemed to sag with relief.

"You thought I was reaching for a knife, didn't you?" I said in a whisper. "You thought I was going to kill you."

"No, no, of course not. What a ridiculous idea. Why on earth should I think that?" I knew he was lying. Paul Stafford was a Graznian prince, stalked by fanatics bent on assassination. When I said I knew who he was in an empty room and reached inside my jacket right afterward, he'd been terrified.

"You're not Paul Stafford at all, are you?" I said gently.

"Listen to me, Iris." He grabbed my hands, holding them tightly. I wasn't sure if he was simply carried away by the emotion of the moment, or if he was trying to prevent my reaching for a weapon. "Listen to me carefully. My life has been worthless. There's only one thing in it that's of any importance to me, and that's my music. I want to go to Chicago. I want to be the best white jazz pianist in the world. Nothing can stop me from trying. Not Rasneski, not you, nobody."

"How can Rasneski stop you?" I said.

"He's threatened to break my fingers," said Paul. "Not personally, of course." He laughed nervously. "But I can well imagine he'd carry out the threat. And my dream would vanish. I'm not going to let him kill my dream."

"Are you a prince?" I said, exasperated.

"How absurd," he said softly. He released my hands. "A

prince of a country that does not exist. It's a twisted idea of Rasneski's."

"Why won't you tell me?"

"What good would that do?" he said sadly. "Would it bring back Mr. Twist?"

"No, but it might help solve his murder."

"As far as I'm concerned," said Paul Stafford, "a prince of Graznia was stabbed to death in a deck chair. The drama is over. And Paul Stafford is a piano player with a future. Iris, all I want to do is to make music and get away from Rasneski."

"You won't admit it," I said.

"The prince is dead," said Paul firmly. He seemed to have regained his composure. "Now tell me, Iris, how long has it been since you decided I was a prince?" He stroked my hair. "Is that why you kissed me last night? Because you thought I was a prince?" He smiled a sad little smile.

"I kissed you because you kissed me first," I said. "And I didn't think you were a prince then."

"We'll see if it makes any difference whether I'm a prince or not," he said, and he kissed me again. After a rather delicious interlude during which I completely forgot about the case, I regained my senses and pushed him away.

"But Mr. Twist is dead," I said with a little sob. "Doesn't that mean anything to you?"

Paul shrugged. "I didn't kill him. I'd never seen him before."

"But you knew who Rasneski was," I said. "You *must* be the prince. And if you are, your life is still in danger."

"Only if word gets out that I'm a prince," said Paul. "And if that does happen, it will ruin my career as well. Who will ever listen to my music and take it for what it is? No one. People will simply say, 'There is a prince who plays the piano.'"

Someone loomed up behind me. It was Jack Clancy. "I don't know, Stafford," he said. "Might come in real handy.

Might give an ordinary piano player a little something extra.
Like publicity. Might make it easier to get a job."

"Jack!" I exclaimed, wondering how much he'd seen and
heard.

"Sorry to interrupt, Iris," he said smoothly. "Your aunt is
looking for you, and I said I'd help her find you." He turned
to Paul and smiled. "Really, I think a piano player with blue
blood would be a real success back home."

"Leave him alone!" I said to Jack.

"Did he send you here to ask me these things, Iris?" said
Paul coldly. "Have the two of you been playing at detectives?
What a charming companion you've recruited, Mr. Clancy.
What you can't find out, a pretty girl can."

"Paul!" I cried.

He looked at me with a melancholy scowl. "Leave me now,
both of you," he said. "I have to practice." He went to the
piano and began his gloomy chords again. There had been
something regal in his dismissal of us.

I took Jack's arms and practically dragged him from the
room. "How *could* you?" I said. "You gave me twenty-four
hours."

"I was worried about you," said Jack. "After I left, it occurred to me that Paul Stafford could easily be one of these
Comrades of the New Dawn. What better way to deflect
suspicion from himself than by pretending to be the intended victim?"

"How absurd," I said. I knew that it wasn't true. Paul Stafford was a prince. He'd been clearly frightened when I'd
reached for the chain of my locket after telling him I knew
who he really was. He'd known he was an assassin's target.
But I didn't tell Jack any of that. I was too angry with him.

"Is my aunt really looking for me?" I said, seething.

"No. I made that up," he said. "I thought you might need
rescuing."

"I don't," I said. "How much did you hear?"

"Not much. Just that he said he didn't want to be a prince.

Which in my book means he probably is." Jack turned to me rather vehemently. "But even if he is, it doesn't give him license to grab any attractive girl he wants and kiss her like that. What a nerve."

"Oh, Jack," I said. "It's just that—"

"Skip it, Iris. You don't owe me any explanations." He took my arm and seemed to regain his old jauntiness. "What else did you get out of him? Besides a pass, I mean. Let's find a cozy little place for an uninterrupted chat." He led me to the ship's library, which was completely empty. Even the auburn-haired conductress was absent.

"I take it you think he's the prince," he said as we settled down in two oak chairs at a small table. "What a story."

"Stop it," I said. "If he is, and you tell the world about it, it could ruin his life. He's serious about a musical career. And you'd put him in mortal danger as well."

"Well, maybe Probrislow will line up some other sap to take the next knife for him," said Jack. His gray-green eyes grew cold.

"I don't believe he had anything to do with that," I said. "That is, if he is the prince. Oh, Jack, it's all so complicated. I don't know what to think."

"Well, I think there's a good chance this Twist fellow died because one of these assassin fellows thought he was the prince. He was traveling with Baron Rasneski. And he had that blue ring. Why would he have that ring?"

"Probrislow, I mean Rasneski, gave it to him," I said with a sick, hollow feeling.

"So an assassin would think Twist was the prince," said Jack triumphantly. "What a story. As soon as we get to Montreal—"

"No," I said. "You can't. Not until the killer is caught. You can't put Paul Stafford in danger."

"He doesn't seem to care that Twist was set up," said Jack. "Let's face it, your prince has feet of clay. He's no good, Iris."

"I don't want to hear this," I said, and I realized with a shock that I was near tears. "He's a tortured young man, he's—" I stopped.

"Oh, forget it, Iris. Stop apologizing for him. You know, there's a fine chance he isn't the prince at all. He could be the killer, just like I told you. Diverting suspicion from himself by pretending to be the prince."

"That's crazy," I said.

"Well, these Comrades sound plenty crazy. Or," said Jack, "he could be trying to get everyone to think he's a prince so he'll be more interesting. I can't think of a vaudeville act with a better angle than a European title."

"He seems awfully serious about his music," I said feebly.

"Yeah, well, I've heard his music, and it's awfully serious," said Jack.

"And what about the blackmailer?" I said. "There still might be something in that. Maybe Vera Nadi *did* get a blackmail note. Rasneski says Twist was a known blackmailer."

Jack looked thoughtful. "It's possible," he said slowly. "How does this sound? Rasneski gets this fellow right out of jail and plans to use him as a decoy in order to save the real prince. But the patsy turns out to be a blackmailer and goes right to work, managing in the process to get himself bumped off. What do you think?"

"It could be even worse than that," I said. "Rasneski could have killed him himself so that whoever is after the real prince thinks the job's already been done."

"Aha!" said Jack. "You do think Paul Stafford is the real prince."

I did, but I denied it. "Not necessarily. He certainly didn't admit it. Anyway, if he is and it gets out, he could be killed. Promise me you won't tell a soul about any of this until we learn more? Please, Jack?"

"I'll hold off awhile more," he replied. "I want a story, but

I'm not as cavalier about murder as your friend Paul Stafford seems to be. I don't want to see a second killing."

We heard a delicate cough. The ship's conductress was standing there, looking severe. Jack had been leaning close to me across the table during our conversation.

"Miss Cooper," she said in her cozy burr, "I hope you aren't the subject of unwanted attentions in the library!"

Jack looked horrified. "Absolutely not," he said.

CHAPTER TEN

*I*t must have been dawn when I heard the scream; the sky through the porthole was gray streaked with scarlet. It was a subdued scream, but a scream nevertheless, and it had come from the passage. Aunt Hermione slept.

I stepped into the passage and set my bare foot into a pool of soapy water. A maid stood screaming, staring into the small steward's cabin farther down the corridor, a fallen mop at her side.

I rushed forward and went into the cabin. Hawkins, the cabin steward, his blond, lanky head thrust back, his eyes frozen in terror, his mouth open in a silent cry of anguish, lay dead.

"Fetch the captain at once," I said sharply to the maid, whose screams were now quiet sobs. "Can you manage that?" I looked at her carefully.

"Yes," she sniffed. Given something to do, she would manage quite well, I thought.

I stepped carefully into the cabin, holding my kimono about me, attempting to disturb nothing, yet endeavoring to observe as much as possible. I heard muffled voices from the adjoining cabins and pulled the door quietly closed. No sense in attracting a crowd, I thought.

Hawkin's cabin had been searched, and searched ruthlessly. Drawers had been pulled out, papers tossed into heaps, twisted piles of clothing cast into the sink. The corpse itself, sprawled unnaturally on the bed, was littered with

127

cheap magazines and tattered paper-covered books. The mattress had been pulled away, and the whole scene was a screaming, crazy composition of crooked angles.

Swallowing hard, I bent over the corpse. It lay partly on its side, as if it had been pulled forward at some point during the search. Neatly in the lower back, the brass hilt of a paper knife gleamed. But this time the blood around the hilt was less vivid. It looked congealed. I began to feel dizzy. Remembering to disturb nothing, I fought the impulse to lean against something and stood purposefully erect, fixing my gaze on a picture on the opposite wall in an attempt to maintain my equilibrium.

It depicted a young lady stepping into a marble pool in transparent robes. It was a cheap sort of thing, relying on a vaguely classical look to justify its fleshy appeal. It looked so silly, hanging there above the chaos in the cabin. I got a vivid impression of poor Hawkins admiring it before he dozed off.

But why did it hang there so squarely and undisturbed. At once, I remembered my cousin Louise. When we were fourteen or so, she had shown me a collection of very foolish letters from the grocer's boy. Louise wasn't a very intelligent girl, but she possessed the kind of sneaky shrewdness that often accompanies a less than powerful intellect. She had hidden her letters in the frame of an engraving of Pocahontas that hung in her bedroom.

I reached for the print of Diana or whoever it was very carefully, using my kimono sleeves to avoid smudging any fingerprints, even though the picture did look untouched. Turning it over, I noticed a faint bulge in the cardboard backing. I twisted the bent nails that held the backing in place and lifted off the cardboard.

I found an envelope. It contained American, Canadian, and English notes in small amounts, and a folded piece of paper that seemed to be some kind of crude ledger, with figures written next to short phrases:

A gentleman who's losing his wife's money at cards.
Gold Stickpin.
His boss might like to know he did a stretch. £5.
Someone seen coming out of the wrong stateroom.
Governess is light-fingered.
Unsuitable reading for a young lady.
Physician, heal thyself. £10. 2 bottles good whiskey.
An indiscreet past. Royal hijinks.

Hawkins, it appeared, had been our blackmailer. The
notes were sketchy, and the amounts pitifully small. Hawkins had obviously operated a small-potatoes sort of business, a one-time-only payment, and a small one, to avoid real
trouble; more a nasty nuisance than anything else.

The captain came into the cabin. "Good Lord, not another
one! Oh, my God!" He passed a hand over his forehead and
frowned at me. "What are you doing here? Where's that girl,
Clara?"

"I'm not coming in," said the maid from the passage.

"Go fetch Colonel Marris," he said.

"Yes, sir."

"Really, Miss Cooper, this is much too trying. Thank God
Marris is here. I'm a sailor, not a policeman."

"What kind of a policeman is Colonel Marris exactly?" I
asked.

"What? Oh. Listen, Miss Cooper, you must get back to
your cabin. Leave this to Marris. Don't ask questions. Everything's well in hand," he added unconvincingly, taking in the
scene around him.

Colonel Marris, dressed in a most uncharacteristic dressing gown of flamboyant maroon silk with lots of gold frogs
and tassels, burst into the cabin. "What's all this, then?" he
demanded.

"Hawkins is dead," I said. "And he was the blackmailer." I
handed him the ledger. "Can't imagine how whoever con-

ducted this search missed this. I was just asking the captain exactly what sort of policeman you are," I added eagerly.

The colonel shot the captain a look of disgust.

"Who found the body?" the colonel asked.

"The maid, Clara, on her early morning rounds," said the captain.

"And I found the maid," I said. "And I sent her for the captain and stayed here, making sure nothing was disturbed. I haven't touched a thing, really I haven't, except for this picture. I found the list and the bank notes behind it."

Colonel Marris consulted the paper I'd handed him for the first time. After a moment, he said, "Hmm. Nasty fellow. Small amounts, thought he was making it safe for himself."

"But he was wrong," I said.

"Quite," muttered the colonel.

"You mean an employee of the line was blackmailing the passengers?" said the captain, the unpleasant knowledge dawning slowly on his handsome face. "Oh no, it can't be. There must be some mistake. See here, Marris, can't we keep this hushed up? They won't like it in London. Won't like it a bit. I never did like Hawkins. Unctuous fellow. But I never dreamed . . ." He trailed off and began to pull nervously at his spade-shaped beard.

Colonel Marris leaned over the body. "Brutish business," he muttered.

"Oh dear," said the captain, in a voice an octave higher than his normal voice. "I suppose we'll have to form another committee. I have other duties to attend to. I cannot bear the strain. The company will—"

"I think," said the colonel calmly, "that under the circumstances, another inquiry of that sort won't be necessary. Poor Twist died rather publicly, and our inquiries were designed to soothe the passengers as much as anything else. I think we should make as little as possible of this second murder. Have the doctor see to the body, and keep the room sealed. The young lady seems to have found the most im-

portant thing in it. The clue to the killer," he added omin-
ously, "may be in this list."

"Hawkins's notes weren't much more than shorthand," I
said. "But we can probably piece together something. The
man losing at cards, for instance. I'm sure that's Captain
Fitzhugh."

"How do you know?" asked the colonel sharply.

"Well, this business about the stickpin. Captain Fitzhugh
was missing a stickpin. His wife thought the governess
might have taken it, but Captain Fitzhugh defended Fräulein
Reiter without telling his wife what really happened to it—
that he'd given it to Hawkins. Poor fellow, I guess Hawkins
knew he didn't have cash. What a bad character Hawkins
was."

"Then this bit about the light-fingered governess—"
mused the colonel, tapping Hawkins's notes.

"Hawkins was on the wrong track there, I imagine," I said,
and I explained how Hawkins had been nearby when Mrs.
Fitzhugh had connected the missing stickpin with Fräulein
Reiter. "Probably heard just a scrap of the conversation and
decided to pursue the blackmail angle with poor Fräulein
Reiter."

"Yes," said the colonel. "It fits. Hawkins was a clumsy
sort of blackmailer. Picked up odd bits of conversation here
and there, fragments of conversation, like the story Judge
Griffin told about Vera Nadi. Probably went through
people's things, too."

I shuddered, mentally running through my possessions,
wondering what incriminating thing Hawkins might have
found. I thought of the purple-bound copy of Elinor Glyn's
Three Weeks hidden under my underthings in my wardrobe
trunk, and realized one of Hawkins's entries might have
been applied to me. Perhaps he'd died before he'd had a
chance to blackmail me. I blushed, and the colonel noticed.

"Damned unpleasant," he said. "Can't say I feel too sorry
for the fellow. Still, I can't imagine what aspect of his sordid

activities led him to this grisly end. There's no doubt in my mind that it's the work of the same killer. Stabbed in the same place, and with a ship's paper knife. How many of them are there lying around, for God's sake? Can't imagine collecting them all up will do much good."

"They're mostly lying around on writing tables, in the library and in the social hall," I said. "You don't expect another murder, do you?"

"There is that possibility," said the colonel grimly. "I certainly didn't expect more than one. But each murder gives us a better opportunity to learn the killer's identity." He seemed to cheer up at this last thought.

"Let us hope," I remarked stiffly, "that a third brutal slaying will not be necessary to establish the final clues that will lead to the murderer's apprehension." Colonel Marris, I decided, took murder too lightly.

He seemed not to notice my disapproval. "Hawkins here must surely have tumbled to something to do with the first murder. Perhaps he even saw it. But murder would have been too dangerous for him. I can't imagine him having the nerve required to blackmail a murderer. Hawkins may have been stupid, but he was not that stupid, surely."

"Unless," I said slowly, "he saw something to do with the murder that he didn't connect with the murder. He did seem to get his facts jumbled. And then blackmailed the killer for the wrong reason."

"Hmm." The colonel consulted Hawkins's list. "Could be. Perhaps this entry about someone coming out of the wrong stateroom."

"Well, I think we can imagine what *that* refers to," I said, blushing.

"Oh. Yes. Rather." The colonel seemed unruffled.

"Good morning, boys and girls," said a cheery voice from the doorway. It was Jack Clancy. He was wearing an elegant navy blue silk robe over white silk pajamas. I reflected on the sartorial splendor of these two bachelors. Father, an old-fashioned man, always wore starched white nightshirts with a simple monogram on the pocket.

"Oh, my God. He's dead," said Jack in a solemn, hushed tone. I'd never seen him look so serious. A second later he was his old breezy self. "Who found the body?" he said, his eyes bright.

"Good Lord, Clancy," barked the colonel. "What are you doing here? And do you know anything about this? What did you know about Hawkins? Or Twist, for that matter? Eh?"

"I'll be glad to tell you, colonel. Just as I'm sure you'll be glad to tell me all about this setup. Well, it seems Twist was a jailbird. And I got it from Hawkins here." He gestured toward the corpse in a rather hesitant way that belied his brash tone. "It didn't come cheap, either, I'll tell you that. Hawkins had some long-winded story about his cousin's having been in the calaboose with Twist, but if you ask me, Hawkins did a stretch himself. Anyway, this Twist wasn't supposed to have been big-time—just a sneak thief who got caught the first time out. Kind of a sad case."

"So Hawkins plied some of his nasty goods to you, did he?" said the colonel.

"I bought it, fair and square. I didn't know he was our blackmailer." Jack paused expectantly, as if waiting for an answer.

"Yes, yes," said the colonel irritably. "He was indeed our blackmailer. What else did you learn from him?"

"Not much. Hawkins wasn't what you'd call an informed source. Picked up a lot of junk and tried to peddle it like it was the goods. That Nadi story, hell, the judge had blathered that one around the night before Hawkins tried to sell it to me. But somehow this thing about Twist's doing time had the ring of truth. I was interested in finding out who killed Twist and why. So I bought it. Hawkins got all glittery-eyed telling me, like it was one of his better items. Then later the professor said something similar about Twist's shady past. Somehow I think Hawkins might have been a more reliable source.

"What made you come rushing here just now?" demanded the colonel.

"Clara's such a helpful girl," said Jack. "And she knows I take a great interest in shipboard happenings. You know, I'm planning to give her a generous tip. My room's always done up clean as a whistle."

"You Americans," hissed the colonel, "think you can buy anything."

"Well, some people thought they could buy Hawkins's silence," said Jack. With his head craned sideways, he was attempting to read the blackmail ledger the colonel held in his hand.

"I'm surprised," snapped the colonel, "that with all your other professional skills, you haven't also mastered the trick of reading upside down."

"Miss Cooper," said Jack irreverently, "can this be you? 'Unsuitable reading for a young lady'? Did Hawkins catch you reading Captain Billy's *Whiz Bang* after lights out?" He laughed heartily at this sally. "Let's see, 'indiscreet past' must be the Nadi dame, and the doctor's here, of course. 'Wrong stateroom'? Was that the best he could do? As a blackmailer, Hawkins was a good cook. Why, he didn't get a thing on me. A disappointing list altogether. Doesn't say 'seen murdering on the promenade deck' anywhere."

"Listen, Clancy," said the colonel. "I don't like your manner. I don't like providing you with copy for your wretched newspaper. But I do appreciate any information you can provide, and you are indeed tenacious and uncannily successful in your pursuit of information. I can only ask you to come forward with anything you know. And I request that you keep things quiet here on board. No sense riling people up, and the passengers are no doubt jittery enough as it is. We're going to keep this second murder as quiet as possible. And for your own safety, I think I should remind you we have a killer on the loose. A killer who has killed twice, and who is no doubt willing to kill again. So be careful."

"You a dick for the line?" Jack asked.

"Let's just say this is rather a busman's holiday," said the colonel. "Now let's all get back to our cabins. I imagine the passage is empty."

"Not so fast, colonel," said Jack. "I think it's time for a little chat."

"Here? Now?" Colonel Marris rolled his eyes in the direction of the corpse.

"Why not? We won't be disturbed. You just said I should tell you what I know. If you're somebody official, and you're square, I'd like to do just that."

Jack gave the captain an inquiring look. The colonel nodded to the captain. "Go ahead," he said.

"Colonel Marris is a representative of the Foreign Office," said the captain. "The directors of the Blue Star Line wired me that information in code and asked that I give him the run of the ship. No one among the passengers or crew is aware of his real identity."

"Okay," said Jack. "I'll tell you what I know. But in exchange I'd like to know what you know. About Graznia and the prince. The whole story."

"This is preposterous," sputtered the colonel.

Jack held out his hands. "Okay. You don't have to play ball. But neither do I. Unless you have some way to give me a subpoena. Otherwise, I'm saving everything for the D.A. or whoever's in charge when we get to Montreal."

The colonel thought a minute. He looked very calculating, and then he said, "All right. But there's no need for Miss Cooper—"

"Miss Cooper is a friend and a valued associate," said Jack pleasantly. "And a pretty smart girl, too. A lot of what I know I got from her. So we can speak freely in front of her.

And I'm going to ask you not to worry her aunt about all the clever sleuthing that she's done. I know I can count on your word as a gentleman."

Jack took a short breath, then plunged into his interrogation with the ferocity of a terrier. "Now, why were you so keen to tell me about these Comrades of the New Dawn? Are you on their trail?"

"That's right," said the colonel. "And I thought it best to let the quarry know what was afoot. I wanted them to realize they had a good chance of being caught if they tried anything irregular. So I talked it up a bit."

"Why are you on this vessel?" said Jack.

"We learned one of their agents was to be aboard," said the colonel. "Later I found that Rasneski would be on board. Adviser to Prince Ludovic."

"Ludovic?" I said. "The prince's name is Ludovic?"

"Yes. He sailed on this vessel, too, God rest his soul. That story of Hawkins's and Rasneski's is ridiculous. A screen. Mr. Twist wasn't a common criminal.

"Amazing as it may seem, it appears to me that the baron posed as Probrislow, and the prince accompanied him as his secretary, Mr. Twist. Agents of a certain society—"

"The Comrades of the New Dawn," I said.

"Yes. It appears that agents of the New Dawn penetrated the prince's incognito and assassinated him. We had information that this attempt would take place. Rasneski is an elusive man. He and this prince, Prince Ludovic, have been underground for years, while Rasneski plotted a return to the throne. His majesty was a mere lad of sixteen when the monarchy toppled ten years ago in 1917." The colonel looked very tired.

"I am telling you this because you have pieced together so much, and because you will not stop until I tell you what I know. And it would be dangerous for you to pursue the matter.

"I was sent to protect the prince. Of course, I had a job of it, I can tell you. I had no current photographs of Rasneski or the prince; as I say, they've been incognito for years, appearing officially only at the most exclusive functions of exiled Graznians. I knew only that they would be sailing on this vessel, on their way to New York, where wealthy Graznian-Americans stood ready to finance a new effort to restore the monarchy. And I had information that the Comrades were planning to assassinate the prince on the high seas. With him out of the way, they felt freer to establish their own Graznian nationalist movement, and their own revolution, according to their own nefarious social theories."

The colonel sighed. "And I failed. Frankly, I never dreamed it was Twist. Can't imagine anyone with less regal bearing. Rasneski is a clever man; he trained his royal charge well in the art of deceit. But Twist was Prince Ludovic, all right. The description tallies exactly. Five feet eleven inches, dark hair, blue eyes. Twenty-six years old. And the ring clinches it."

"But why did the British government want to protect Prince Ludovic?" I said. It was an absurd name, I thought.

"His majesty is a cousin of my own king," said the colonel gravely.

"It's incredible," I murmured. "Mr. Twist, a prince." I avoided Jack's eye. I didn't want to tell Paul's secret just yet.

"A king, actually," said the colonel. "The coronation was a hasty affair, just ahead of a mob. The king was smuggled out of the country just in advance of a rebellion. The old king had abdicated after the scandal with Rosa Nadescu, Vera Nadi now, and this Twist fellow was a nephew. But the scandal had turned the people against the whole monarchy. A shame to see a perfectly good form of government ruined by one unsuitable monarch. These Graznians are a hot-blooded bunch.

"Rasneski's been scheming for years to get the old lot back in, but without a king it'll be rough going. After all, the country itself's been off the map for years."

"Who succeeds Mr. Twist?" said Jack. "I can't quite call the fellow Prince Ludovic," he added, giving me a significant look.

"Probably some cousins about," said the colonel wearily. "These peculiar little dynasties can be quite complicated. But it's really a moot point now, I'd say."

Jack turned to me. "Iris," he said softly, "don't you think there's something you should tell the colonel, now that you know his mission was to protect the prince?"

"Must I?" I said, although I knew I should.

"You were supposed to tell me what *you* found out," said the colonel irritably to Jack. "I took it that you gave me your word of honor as a gentleman."

"Well," said Jack, "I didn't find out anything. Iris did. And I kind of gave her my word of honor as a gentleman, that is, I implied—"

"Oh, be quiet, both of you," I said. "Listen, Colonel Marris, I don't think Twist was a prince at all. I think Paul Stafford is a prince—the ship's piano player. I think Rasneski lured that pathetic Mr. Twist to his death, using him as a decoy."

The colonel's face grew white. "Why do you think that?" he said.

"Well, mostly," I said, steering away from the personal, "there's the postage stamp. Here, I'll show you." I fished my locket out from under my nightdress, opened it, and handed him the Graznian stamp from little Bobby Fitzhugh's collection.

Colonel Marris squinted at the pale blue stamp. Beneath a smudge of postmark, it bore the profile of a man with a classic nose and a smooth brow. "Probably the old king. Too bad we can't see the date on this thing, but as I say, the place disappeared in 1917, so it's at least that old. I can't imagine they had time to get up a new lot of stamps in the midst of a revolution and with the new king on his way into exile.

"Besides," he added, "these things never look like the real chaps anyway. You saw Twist. Can't have a bust of a weasely-looking monarch on your stamps. I imagine they just knock off a copy of some old Roman or Greek. Your whole theory about this piano player is based on this postage stamp?" said the colonel.

"Well, Paul Stafford seems to know something," I said vaguely. "He knew Rasneski." I felt horrid. If Paul was Prince Ludovic, or King Ludovic for that matter, and he wanted to be just plain Paul Stafford, why shouldn't he be allowed to do just that? "You aren't going to talk to him about this, are you, colonel?"

"Do you think, perhaps," said the colonel gently, "that you don't think the piano player is King Ludovic simply because he's such a handsome young man and it would be rather charming if he were a king?"

Jack gave me a malicious look of triumph.

"Of course not," I said huffily. Actually I was pleased. Colonel Marris hadn't taken me seriously and Paul's secret was salvaged if not saved.

Now the colonel turned to Jack Clancy. "This is it? This is the trove of information you have to tell me? That Twist wasn't the prince but the ship's pianist was?"

"If I were you," said Jack, "I'd pursue that angle. What are you going to do?"

"Hmm? Never you mind. I'm waiting for new developments. Nothing that need concern you."

"You must have an agent working with the Comrades of the New Dawn," said Jack. "After all, you knew that they'd have one of their boys aboard and that they'd be trying to kill the king of Graznia. Boy, what a story."

"There'll be nothing to publish until we get to Montreal," said the colonel. "Meanwhile," he said, indicating Hawkins's sprawling corpse, "it's in everyone's best interest that the passengers and crew know of little of this as possible."

"We have a large deep freeze on board," said the captain. "I'm sure the doctor can arrange something discreetly."

"But what about poor Hawkins?" I said. "What about him? Who killed him? A blackmail victim, or one of the Comrades of the New Dawn?"

"I shall do my very best to find out," said the colonel. "Now let us all go back very quietly to our cabins."

CHAPTER ELEVEN

After breakfast, Jack Clancy cornered me. "This is getting pretty serious," he said. "Just what we feared. A second murder."

"Yes," I said. "You know, Jack, Hawkins and Twist were strangely similar, as far as we know: both unprepossessing young men apparently with criminal tendencies. But unpleasant as they may have been, they both had a right to live. They should not have been cut down in such a cavalier manner."

"Absolutely," said Jack. "And they mustn't go unavenged. We've got to find out who killed them. And I bet we can. By the way, Iris, did you tell your aunt about Hawkins?"

"No, I didn't." I felt guilty about this, but I knew there was no way Aunt Hermione would be discreet. And the captain and Colonel Marris had wanted everything kept quiet. "I didn't want to upset her," I said. "Do you think the colonel will solve the mystery?"

Jack shrugged. "He didn't seem to take your Paul Stafford story seriously. But then you didn't tell him everything, either. All his dire warnings and veiled statements."

"I can't imagine what Paul meant," I said. "I can't think it matters too much. Perhaps it was just an attempt on his part to make himself seem dangerous and interesting," I said in a tone of amused sophistication.

"But you're too smart to fall for that sort of thing, aren't you?" said Jack brightly. "All right. Let's start detecting right now. Let's go pay Sparks a visit."

"The wireless officer?"

"Sure. Let's see what Marris got from land. He's sent a couple of Marconigrams. Might be something in 'em."

The telegrapher was a spidery young man with a shock of dark hair and a humorous mouth.

"I can't let you see copies of the communications sent from this ship," he said. "So don't ask me to." But he winced a little, as if he were afraid he'd give in.

"I can appreciate that," said Jack kindly. "And under ordinary circumstances, I wouldn't ask you. But it's this way." He sat on the desk and assumed a confidential manner, hooking his thumbs in his waistcoat pockets. "Are you a betting man?" he inquired.

"Get to the point," replied the young man.

"This young lady here, Miss Cooper . . ." I smiled with as much dazzle as I could muster. "She and I have a little friendly wager going."

The telegrapher eyed me dubiously.

"She says the colonel is just what he appears to be, a retired military man. But I'm sure he's a reporter for one of your English papers. I *swear* I saw the fellow in London covering the same match I covered. Say, what a fight! Our man clobbered the guy. 'Course, let's face it, we Americans just breed better fighters. Parkinson was the best you had, but he was no match for Dorrity, no sir. Anyway . . . say, mind if I . . ." Jack helped himself to a cigarette from a box on the desk. "Do you mind? Thanks. Obliged. Anyway, I was telling Miss Cooper here that this fellow calling himself Marris is a reporter, but he's keeping it quiet so he can scoop the world on this deck chair murder. But she didn't believe me. Told me to put my money where my mouth was. I hate to disappoint the lady; Miss Cooper's an awfully nice girl, but I'm right. And I told her these Marconigrams he's been sending are stories he's sending his paper."

"Well, the lady wins," said the telegrapher with malicious satisfaction. "The colonel's telegrams are all to a firm of im-

porters, and they're strictly business. I'm sure you're accustomed to being right, but you're wrong."

"Pay up," I said brightly.

"Hold your horses," said Jack. "Let's have a look at 'em.
Sparks here is just being gallant. Or maybe Marris slipped
him a couple a' bills."

"Oh, honestly," snapped the telegrapher, and rummaged
in a drawer. "Here are the copies, see for yourself." He
handed Jack a fistful of flimsy carbon copies.

The clatter of the wire began, and while the telegrapher
took the message, Jack and I raced through the telegrams.

The afternoon of Mr. Twist's murder, Colonel Marris had
sent the following wire:

> OUR COMPETITORS SUCCESSFUL STOP CARGO DAMAGED
> BEYOND REPAIR STOP SHIPPING NUMBER 51126 STOP BROWN
> AND BLUE STOP MARRIS

And he had received the following reply:

> YOUR DESCRIPTION DAMAGED CARGO TALLIES STOP OFFICIAL
> IDENTIFICATION MUST WAIT UNTIL OUR CANADIAN BRANCH
> TAKES CHARGE STOP CHIEF MOST DISAPPOINTED STOP BLACK
> DAY FOR THE FIRM STOP BLUE STAR INFORMED OF GRIEVOUS
> NATURE OF CARGO DAMAGE AND WILL COOPERATE WITH YOU
> STOP BAD LUCK MARRIS STOP SMETHURST

Some days later, the colonel had sent another wire to the
import firm.

> DOING BEST TO UNTANGLE STOP AWARE OF GRAVITY OF
> SITUATION STOP TAKE FULL RESPONSIBILITY STOP ANY NEW
> INFORMATION HELPFUL STOP MARRIS

> LATEST INFORMATION TRANSACTION TO HAVE BEEN
> HANDLED BY YOUNG AMERICAN AGENT STOP NO MORE PAR-
> TICULARS STOP CHIEF APPARENTLY CONSIDERING YOUR
> POSSIBLE TRANSFER TO OUR ICELANDIC BRANCH STOP GOOD
> LUCK OLD THING STOP SMETHURST

"Well, say, this is a pushover," said Jack. "I was afraid we'd have to waste time with some code. This must be all about the Comrades and the prince. Poor Twist here is damaged goods. This shipping number is his description, see? Five feet eleven, twenty-six years old, that fits with his passport, and brown hair and blue eyes.

"Marris's bosses seem to have decided this was the prince. That's what 'description tallies' means. Poor old Marris seems to be in hot water. Say, don't these civil servants waste the public's money, though? All this stuff about the chief! Sounds as bad as my editor. But what's this about 'young American agent'?"

"That can only mean the assassin," I replied. "See, it says 'transaction *to have been* handled' by their American agent. It's a completed action in the past. The Comrades of the New Dawn's agent is an American."

"That means you or me, sweetheart," said Jack softly. "We were on deck, and we're young Americans. And I still feel only someone seen on deck could have done the deed."

He paused. It was an uncomfortable moment. "I know I didn't do it, and I bet you didn't either, right?" he asked.

I nodded. "There must be some other explanation," I said. I toyed with the idea of Jack being an assassin for the Comrades of the New Dawn. It didn't seem to fit.

"I'm forthright," he had once said, and I believed him. Yet there was nothing forthright about our killer. Secret stabbings were just plain sneaky. Of course, Jack was clever, but if he were the assassin, why should he draw such attention to himself, pursuing the case so zealously? The killer could only do that if he were callously arrogant. But then, I mused, the killer had to be arrogant. Murder, deciding for another when his life will end, was the ultimate arrogance.

Jack watched my face as these thoughts raced through my mind. Did he know I was suspecting him?

"Aw, you think I'm the guy," he said gently. "I know you

do. Well, for what it's worth, I don't think you're the assassin, even though I know I'm not, and you were the only other young American on deck. Because, Iris, you're square." He smiled. "And I don't blame you, even if you think I am the guy," he added loyally.

"Gee, Jack, the cable must mean something else," I said.

"Well, we got two whole days to figure this thing out, don't we?" said Jack optimistically. "We'll crack this case. You watch."

I hoped Jack was right. But I wasn't as optimistic. We had just two more days.

CHAPTER TWELVE

"*O*h, Iris." My after-breakfast stroll was interrupted by a girlish shriek. Ursula Destinoy-Pinchot hurried toward me. "Oh, Iris, I know we've just met, but I must confide in you. I need your help." I eyed Ursula uneasily. Her cheeks were a vivid pink, her eyes had a sparkle that had hitherto eluded them, and she had a spring in her step and a flutter to her lashes I hadn't noticed before. Ursula looked like a girl in love. A quick survey of the details of her costume confirmed this suspicion. Her sensible tweed coat and skirt had been enhanced by a flourish of chiffon scarf, her sensible cloche hat had been pulled down at a more coquettish angle, and she wore a vivid flower in her lapel. Small things, true, but together very telling. Ursula saw herself somewhat differently than she had when we had last met.

"Iris, I hope you'll understand. I've met, well, I've met *a man*, and I don't want Mummy to be upset. I've told her I spent last evening with you and some friends, very late, at charades. And I hope you won't mind. Mummy's ever so strict, not like your Aunt Hermione at all."

I frowned. It was pretty nervy of Ursula to use me as an alibi without consulting me. I shuddered at the thought of a confrontation with her formidable mother.

I was mentally phrasing some tactful objection to his plan, and Ursula rushed on.

"He is marvelous, simply marvelous. I didn't know life could be like this." She sighed happily. "Mummy would never understand. For one thing"—Ursula lowered her voice—"he's a foreigner. And he hasn't a farthing. But he has

147

breeding. And breeding will tell." She twirled a curl coquettishly on her finger.

"Ursula . . ." I began feebly.

"Oh, I must run," she said. "Here he is." And Ursula stood radiant with joy, as the Comte de Lanier came and offered his arm and a dazzling smile. He was indeed handsome, and immaculately dressed. Perhaps too immaculately. I noted with distaste the elaborate arrangement of his breast-pocket handkerchief, and while his scent was no doubt expensive, it had been, I felt, too liberally applied. I sighed as they proceeded slowly down the promenade deck, arm in arm.

Oh well, I thought. Whatever the count's motives, he had done lovely things for Ursula's complexion. And with just one more day left of our cruise, what more harm could he do? The Destinoy-Pinchots were probably not as rich as the Klepps, but perhaps the count was simply keeping his skills sharpened.

I thought idly about these things as I strolled through the passage back to our cabin. Suddenly, the ship took a heavy roll, and I lost my footing and fell toward a cabin door. Unfortunately, the cabin door opened just as I fell toward it, and I careened into the arms of Paul Stafford, who was emerging into the passage. His tie was askew and his hair was ruffled. I apologized, righted myself, and looked into the cabin. There stood Professor Probrislow, appearing equally disreputable, and clutching one eye.

"What are you doing?" I asked.

"I have just planted my fist in the professor's eye," said Paul. "I'm coming to my senses at last."

"Why that's horrible!" I replied, although I really thought Rasneski probably deserved it. "Let me see."

The professor, following some time-honored reflex developed in small boys, surrendered the eye rather proudly to my ministrations.

"Honestly," I exclaimed, "you're behaving like a couple of

children." The eye was beginning to swell. "Nothing for it but to slap a steak on it," I said. "But it'll still be black and blue. Now, what is this all about?"

"Nothing," murmured the professor.

"A matter of honor," said Paul. "Honestly, old man, I am sorry." He offered his hand to Probrislow, who bowed over it in courtly fashion.

"Iris, I know now what I must do," said Paul. "I promise you, everything will be put in order as it should be. Now I must speak to the captain. Iris, you are coming to the fancy masked ball tonight, aren't you? You must. Iris, you are maddeningly attractive. Do you know that? You should." He took me by the shoulders, kissed me, and set off down the hall, whistling.

"Ring for that steak, will you?" I said to Probrislow. I was flustered by this latest development, but a good medical emergency keeps me steady. "And I'll get cold water and we'll splash it just a little. It will hurt some, but I'll be gentle."

"I'm not a bit surprised," said Aunt Hermione when I recounted the incident to her later, omitting Paul Stafford's gallantries and his kiss. "I've never been able to differentiate between the behavior of grown men and small boys. Although why they should strike each other I can't imagine. The professor and the pianist in particular, I mean, not men and boys in general. Well, my dear, how do I look?"

Aunt Hermione and I were preparing for the masked ball. Aunt Hermione, an indefatigable shopper, had collected an amazing number of peculiar souvenirs from which we could fashion costumes. She now wore a brightly colored Egyptian rug around her shoulders, meant to represent a serape, a white shirt and trousers borrowed from the bath steward, tennis shoes, and a large sombrero with bobbles around the brim. "Pancho Villa," she announced matter-of-factly. After some consultation, we decided the addition of fierce moustaches, applied with burnt cork, would add the proper note of menace, and I suggested she remove the pearls she had haphazardly added at the last minute.

I appeared as a gypsy, with a wide skirt, a Brussels lace blouse pulled daringly off one shoulder, a collection of scarves and sashes around my hair and waist, and an Italian silk piano shawl at a sort of oblique angle to everything else. A collection of rather garish Indian jewelry that Aunt Hermione hadn't been able to resist in Madras completed my ensemble. After a little thought, I dug into the remains of our burnt cork and outlined my hazel eyes. Giggling and making adjustments to our costumes, we set off toward the main saloon.

There were the usual number of gentlemen trucked out as ladies, with the aid of mops and plenty of rouge, and the usual number of Hindoos, with artfully arranged turbans and some sort of darkening agent I suspected was furniture oil. The judge seemed quite in character as a Roman senator with a garland of ivy and a toga of sheeting, and Mrs. Griffin as a Roman matron was strikingly regal. Vera Nadi looked as spectacular as I had expected her to look. She wore a closely fitting black gown with lots of jet beading, a black satin cap coming to a dramatic point on her forehead, and a pair of chiffon bat's wings which she fluttered appropriately. She seemed only slightly annoyed when an even more striking costume appeared. Why hadn't I noticed the woman who was Diana before? She was extremely tall, with a handsome carriage. Her bare arms were strong and supple; she wore a pale tunic and a quiver of silver arrows, and her abundant soft hair was caught up with a silver ribbon and ornamented with a silver half moon. Her white domino mask failed to conceal the chiseled Grecian beauty of her face. Could that be Ursula?

Colonel Marris, decked out as some sort of ancient mariner in tattered clothing with a life preserver around his neck, seemed to be taking great enjoyment in the proceedings. He explained that the rubber chicken he carried represented an albatross, and with very little encouragement, the judge began to recite lines from the poem with his golden orator's voice.

"Omar," said his wife dryly, "always stoppeth one of three."

"Look at Mr. Ogle," said Aunt Hermione. "He's obviously brought a costume along, and hasn't improvised from existing materials." She clucked in disapproval. Aunt Hermione and I considered this very bad form, and not at all sporting. Ogle wore the complete uniform of Napoleon, his owllike spectacles adding an unintentional comic note.

"Know why Napoleon kept his hand like this?" he chortled, demonstrating.

"To hold up his trousers," yawned Jack Clancy. "Heard that old wheeze when I was six."

Ogle frowned. "Mr. Clancy, you are not wearing a costume," he added severely. Jack, apparently unable to bring himself to wear fancy dress, wore instead a dinner jacket. He looked rather elegant, actually.

"Hell, I can't stand dressing up. Or wearing paper hats, either," he explained. "Oh, hello, Iris. We're taking a collection to send Ogle here to Elba. How's that for a bright idea? Oh, you look swell in that getup." He surveyed me approvingly. "But what'd you do to your beautiful eyes? Look like a couple of shiners."

"I don't think you're in any position to criticize those of us who've attended this function in the proper spirit," said Mr. Ogle prissily. "Miss Cooper, we missed you at the ship's concert. A very disappointing turnout in general. Why you young people don't appreciate a little old-fashioned fun is beyond me. Why, the committee worked so hard. And it's all for—"

"Yeah, yeah, widows and orphans," said Jack. "Come on, Iris, let's dance."

Jack hummed a few snatches of tango and executed some

fancy maneuvers. "How's that for a swell turn? Picked that up in a . . . well, never mind. Say, it seems a shame, our having such a good time when we still haven't got a line on these killings," he said in more serious tones. "I kept close to the colonel all day. He's up to something."

"Why, Jack Clancy," I said. "I'm astonished."

"Why? You didn't think Colonel Marris would give up like the rest of the committee, did you? He's got his sworn duty to perform. And besides, he doesn't want to get that post in Iceland. Can't say as I blame him."

"No, not that," I said. "I'm astonished at what a terrific dancer you are."

"What's so astonishing about that?" he said with a smile. "Now just relax and I'll show you something terrific." We danced cheek to cheek facing forward, in true tango fashion, and then Jack twirled me and bent me back so low that my head almost touched the floor. All the while he held me perfectly, so I never worried he'd drop me, I just felt thrilled.

He brought me back up slowly and we laughed together. "We'd better look out," he said. "If we're too good the other dancers will clear away and we'll be the floor show. It's happened to me before."

Just then, the dancers around us parted. Paul Stafford marched toward us, through a corridor of bodies. He wore a scarlet uniform, and across his chest was a blue silk sash emblazoned with medals. Probrislow, his eye beginning to develop purplish tinges, followed him. "His majesty, Ludovic of Graznia, wishes to . . ." He paused. "I believe the expression is 'cut in,' " he said unhappily.

"Excuse the disreputable appearance of my equerry," said Paul.

"Well, what do you know," said Jack. " 'Americanized Prince Slams Ivories!' What a story!"

"You don't mind if I cut in, Clancy, do you?" asked Paul.

"Yes," said Jack. "I do. You can't pull rank on me. We're

in international waters. Miss Cooper and I are having a fine time."

"I know it's a bit thick," said Paul. "But it's the colonel's idea. He's a policeman, you know. It's part of his scheme to force the murderer's hand. It's a long story . . ."

"We know all about it," said Jack. "And it's a great story. But can't it wait until we finish this dance?"

"It's the least I could do for that Twist chap," said Paul quietly. "Step aside, Clancy, will you?" He came toward me.

Suddenly the lights went out.

Women screamed. I felt a pair of strong hands push me firmly away. I fell to the ground and was dimly aware of scuffling bodies above me. After what seemed like forever, I heard a low moan and the clatter of metal on the parquet floor. The lights went up again. The orchestra began its frenzied melody.

CHAPTER THIRTEEN

Surrounded by confused dancers, Paul lay in Jack's arms, pale but grinning. There was a crimson streak on his shirt. The colonel and the captain strode forward, pulled Paul to his feet, and took Jack by the shoulders and hustled him away. It all happened in a matter of seconds. The dancers began again, and no one seemed to have realized that anything untoward had happened. I scrambled to my feet and followed the strange procession out onto the deck.

I caught up with them there: the captain and the colonel, Jack and Paul, and the professor. "Stop," I cried. "Where are you going?" I realized how chilly it was on deck, and how dark, and how quiet.

The professor turned to me. "Go away," he hissed. "You are a foolish, meddlesome girl." The men proceeded to the captain's cabin, and I followed them inside.

"Lock the door," said the colonel. I rushed to Paul and tore off his sash. Medals fell musically to the floor. I opened his shirt. A long, shallow gash ran across his chest.

"He'll be all right," I said. "Just a surface wound. But a nasty cut. Should be disinfected."

"Iris," said Paul. "Now I can tell you everything."

"There is no need for that," said the professor.

"Oh, be quiet, Rasneski," said Paul. "You've done enough damage. My uncle should have thrown you out years ago. You're nothing but a low schemer."

I turned to Probrislow. "Is this King Ludovic?" I asked.

"It is indeed," said Probrislow.

"Then who was Twist?" I demanded.

"Just a poor sucker who got set up but good," said Jack.

"That's right, Iris," said Paul. "Rasneski brought him along as a decoy. He knew that a certain group—"

"The Comrades of the New Dawn," I said impatiently.

"Yes," said Paul. He grimaced from the pain. I held my handkerchief against the gash.

"The bleeding is stopping," I said.

"Fortunately, I do not suffer the ailment of my Russian cousins," said Paul. "But let me continue. Rasneski here, a conniving old retainer of my family, arranged for this unfortunate Twist to accompany him in an attempt to draw the attention of the assassin away from me. He had him wear the royal ring, and he chose him for his height, age, and coloring. I didn't know anything about it. But I suspected it. That's why I questioned you about Twist that first night. My suspicions were confirmed when Twist died."

"We had that much figured out," said Jack. "It's awful," he exclaimed. "What a low trick." He glared at Rasneski. "And why didn't you say anything?" he demanded of Paul.

"I didn't know what to do," Paul answered. "It seemed that it was unnecessary to reveal myself then. The assassin would have had his blood and been satisfied. But I meant to tell the authorities in Canada, when we had safely landed."

"Instead, there was a second killing," said Jack.

"Yes. I heard of it. So I decided to reveal myself. At the same time the colonel somehow found me out. It was his idea for me to appear in full dress, complete with sash and medals."

"And about time, too," said Jack. "I suppose you tore the page about the Crespi-Gravensteins out of the *Almanach* to further cover your tracks."

"Yes," said Paul. "I should have acted sooner, I know. I am too much of a coward to have been a good king. I finally had it out with that evil Rasneski and told him I wouldn't go along." Rasneski touched his eye thoughtfully. "I learned that the colonel was an agent of the British government, sent to protect me. Even he was unaware of Rasneski's low scheme."

"I would certainly not have approved of a British subject being put in such jeopardy unknowingly," said the colonel gravely.

"He was simply a common criminal," said Rasneski with impatience. "He was ennobled by his death, allowing the king of Graznia to live."

"There is no king of Graznia," said Paul. "I am Paul Stafford. I am going to Chicago to learn to play piano like the Americans. I will never set foot in Graznia again. There is indeed no more Graznia. Face it, Rasneski, our kind are all through. And perhaps the world will be a better place for it."

"This is great stuff," said Jack eagerly. "Where's my notebook?"

"You can abandon your rather theatrical journalistic pose," said the colonel. "We know who you are. Your people in London talked. We know you are the American agent of the Comrades of the New Dawn."

"Huh?" said Jack. "How do you figure that?"

"Oh, it's patently obvious," said Marris. "You fanatics can't help yourselves. As soon as we dimmed the lights, after establishing the king's identity, you stabbed him. We have the knife"—the colonel displayed a ship's paper knife wrapped in a handkerchief—"and we're sure your prints are on it. We'll find out when we get to Montreal."

"Say, you're on the wrong track," Jack exclaimed. "It's true, I meant to, well, when this fellow showed up all trucked out like that and demanded to dance with Miss Cooper, well, it's true, I got so mad I planned to land my fist on him. I pushed Miss Cooper here out of the way, and pulled back to sock him a good one, and then the lights went out. Next thing I knew, he fell to my feet. When the lights went up, I was down there on the floor, helping him up. And

I saw the knife nearby. I maybe even picked it up. But I never stabbed anybody. And I'm sure as hell not some agent for some society of cranks. I'm a newspaperman."

"Listen," said the colonel. "We know that the assassin was a young American. You and Miss Cooper were the only young Americans on deck when Twist died. If you didn't stab the prince just now, Miss Cooper did. But I'd wager her prints aren't on that knife."

The captain coughed. "I'm afraid nowadays we don't clap people in irons, but perhaps it would be wise if we detained this young man somewhere."

"Not till I get my story," bellowed Jack. "Tell me why I killed Hawkins."

"He must have found out what you were up to," said the colonel. "He was spying around a good deal. We know that."

"Wait," I cried. "You're all wrong. You're all wrong. Jack and I *weren't* the only Americans on deck. I see now!" I leaped up. "Quick, we may be too late. Where's Fräulein Reiter's cabin?"

"The governess?" exclaimed the colonel.

"Knitting," I cried.

Somehow, I managed to round them up, and we rushed to Fräulein Reiter's cabin, leaving Paul behind, attended by Rasneski

"What's all this about?" frowned the colonel. "We haven't any reason to—"

"Knitting!" I exclaimed. "Knitting is like knives and forks. There's an American way and a German way. She knits the American way. I saw her on deck with the child, and I didn't think until now that—"

The colonel knocked sharply on the door. There was no answer. "Open up," he shouted. A minute later he pushed hard on the door, and we all tumbled inside.

The silvery figure of Diana sat at the dressing table. She removed her white mask. The intelligent eyes of Fräulein

Reiter gazed up at us. "Don't wake the children," she said softly, and held a handkerchief to her face. There was a strange smell, as of bitter almonds. "I have failed," she said, without a trace of her accent. "The tyrant still lives. And you have discovered me." She slumped over.

"Cyanide," said the colonel. "We're too late."

"What a story," muttered Jack. "What a story."

CHAPTER FOURTEEN

"**T**hank God this unpleasantness is finished," sighed the captain. "Although my report to the line will be difficult." We sat in the captain's cabin, drinking large brandies. All in all, we made a rather picturesque group, the colonel in his shipwrecked sailor's costume, the prince with his sash and medals askew, me in my gypsy ensemble, and Jack and the man I now knew as Rasneski both looking rumpled and disheveled. The captain, however, remained immaculate. He drew his hand through his beard. "What will I say about Hawkins in my report?"

"Yes," said Jack. "What about Hawkins? Why was he killed?"

"I rather think," I said, "it was all a dreadful mistake. Hawkins tried to blackmail Fräulein Reiter, or whoever she really was. Remember the entry 'Governess is light-fingered'? He had it all mixed up about the stickpin, thinking he'd overheard she'd taken it. Very silly of him, really, because he heard it from Mrs. Fitzhugh, Fräulein Reiter's employer, so there wasn't much point in blackmailing her at all. Fräulein Reiter undoubtedly thought he was referring to something else entirely."

"Doesn't make sense," said the colonel. "Light-fingered doesn't mean murderous."

"The first paper knife," I said. "She probably thought he saw her slip the paper knife off one of the tables in the library or in the social hall."

"Aha!" said the colonel.

161

"But I can't say he was blackmailing the passengers," said the captain fretfully.

"Poor Hawkins," said Jack. "He was a lousy blackmailer. Pathetic stuff. Imagine, that business about the wrong stateroom! Strictly small-time stuff."

The captain appeared to choke on his brandy. "We've got to destroy that list," he said hoarsely.

"I don't understand your concern for such an insignificant little man," said Rasneski. "He was a common criminal."

"No better than you," sneered Paul.

"I wish you could be charged with a crime," said the colonel to Rasneski, who ignored the remark and bent down to gather up the medals that had fallen from Paul's chest when I'd pulled open his shirt.

"Well, I'll do my best to pillory him in the press," said Jack cheerfully.

Rasneski handed the collection of medals to Paul.

Paul smiled. "I won't be needing these anymore," he said. "Although I believe I'll keep this one for a souvenir. The Order of the Silver Falcon. I believe it saved my life. See? It's bent. The knife must have slithered off it. No, wait, I have a better idea. My last royal act. Iris, come here."

There was indeed something royal in this command. I approached, and, despite his weakness, for he was still pale, he stood and pinned the large medal on my blouse. He kissed me rather tenderly on both cheeks, murmured, "For valor," and sank into a faint.

"Send for the doctor," I said. "The strain has done him in. It's just a simple faint, but he should have his cut dressed properly." The colonel went on this errand, and I unceremoniously poured myself another brandy from the captain's decanter. The jumble of events was beginning to take its toll on me, too.

Jack Clancy, however, was still energetic and enthusiastic. "There's just one more thing," he said. "How did she do it?

How did she stab Twist in broad daylight in front of those kids?"

"I think it's all in the testimony," I said. "Little Agnes saw it all. She just didn't know what she saw. 'He took his nap,' she said. Fräulein Reiter arranged his lap robe over him, tucked him in, just as she tucked Agnes and Bobby in every night, and stabbed him at the same time as she tucked. And Bobby was bent over his little sister, who was crying, probably obscuring what little noise there was." I shuddered.

The colonel returned with the doctor; a whiff of smelling salts revived Paul. I knelt over his fallen form. He smiled up at me. "How did you guess my secret, Iris?"

I laughed. "You won't believe it. It's silly, but I saw your face . . . on a postage stamp."

"How can that be?" asked the colonel. "His majesty was only just crowned when he fled. Why would he be on a postage stamp?"

Paul began to laugh. "It's very simple," he said. "The Graznian economy was dependent on postage stamps. They were our biggest export. Even in revolution, we'd be sure to issue a new stamp. We didn't do much else right, but we made sure we had enough postage stamps to satisfy the collectors of the world." And, still laughing, he was helped from the room.

"Oh, Iris dear, where have you been?" asked Aunt Hermione when I finally arrived back at our cabin. "I've received the most frantic communications from Mrs. Destinoy-Pinchot; she can't find Ursula anywhere and she thought she was with you. I'm afraid she thinks you travel with a very fast set, and I'm afraid I was very sharp with her when she made that suggestion."

I flung myself into my aunt's arms. "Oh, dear Aunt Hermione, it's all over," I said, and burst into tears of exhaustion.

"My dear, whatever is the matter?" she asked, alarmed.

"Nothing, nothing," I replied. "Everything's all right now. We've found the killer." And I proceeded to tell her every detail of the conclusion of the case.

"I'm so proud of you, Iris," she said when I'd told her everything. "You are a brave and clever girl." She turned the silver falcon over in her hand. "What an amazing story. No one will ever believe it in Portland. Oh, my, all that nasty burnt cork around your eyes has run down your face. Let me fix it for you." She bathed my face with a cool washcloth, and helped me to bed.

I slept late, and arrived in the dining saloon the next morning too late to breakfast with the others, but Colonel Marris was waiting for me. "I don't know how to thank you, Miss Cooper," he said. "His majesty's government is most appreciative. You're a very clever girl. It was a thorny case. Thorny indeed. Fräulein Reiter was a most daring assassin. If only she'd used her powers for good instead of—" He broke off. "Excuse me, Miss Cooper, I've just noticed something, a routine bit of police work. Excuse me for a moment."

Curious, I followed him across the dining saloon, to where Captain Fitzhugh and Mr. Ogle were deep in conversation.

"Real nice of you, Fitzhugh," said Ogle. "I tell you, I'm relieved. Real nice indeed. I don't mind telling you I hadn't meant to play for such high stakes."

Captain Fitzhugh smiled a wolfish smile. "No trouble at all, dear chap," he said, and tore a bit of pink paper into tiny pieces.

"What's all this, then?" demanded Colonel Marris sharply.

"Hmm? Oh, nothing that need concern you," said Ogle. "Played some cards last night. Private matter."

"Let me guess," said the colonel. "Captain Fitzhugh here had been losing heavily. Then his luck changed. You lost

Heavily. And you gave him a check for a large amount. A very large amount. Which he kindly tore up before your eyes."

"That's right," said Ogle.

Captain Fitzhugh looked uncomfortable.

"Very foolish to play for such high stakes on board ship," said the colonel severely. "Fitzhugh, give him his check back."

Ogle stared incredulously at the shredded bits of pink paper on the table before him.

"Oldest trick in the book," snorted Marris.

"All right, all right," said Captain Fitzhugh irritably. He produced another piece of pink paper and threw it on the table. "I know when I've lost."

"Why, it's my check!" exclaimed Ogle.

"The one he tore up was a dummy," said the colonel. "Perhaps, Mr. Ogle, you'll profit by this mistake, and refrain from playing for high stakes with strangers."

Embarrassed, Captain Fitzhugh rose and left. Mr. Ogle continued to stare at his check with incredulity.

"Poor Hawkins," said the colonel. "Wrong again. Foolishly blackmails Fitzhugh for losing large sums of his wife's money at cards. Eleanor Fitzhugh's people did have a great deal of money at one time, you know. In reality, Fitzhugh is simply employing the common boatman's swindling device: appear to lose heavily before setting up the victim for the last night out. And poor Ogle, a millionaire from Sioux Falls, is the classic victim. Happens time and time again." He shook his head sadly.

Later, on deck, I encountered another drama of a different sort. Rasneski was bowing low over the gloved hand of Vera Nadi. He clicked his heels smartly. "His majesty's compliments, and he regrets that the doctor forbids his exciting himself further. He wishes me to tell you that he was deeply moved by a discussion you had one evening concerning his late uncle. He wishes you to have, as a token of his esteem, this." And Rasneski handed Vera Nadi the grand seal of Graznia, the large ring with the blue stone.

"Madame, this is my last act as a servant of the House of Crespi-Gravenstein. Graznia," he sobbed, "is no more."

"Perhaps you think I killed it," she replied. "What I did was simply the act of a young woman in love. And in a strange way, old enemy, we are very similar. We both loved too much. And we both killed the thing the other loved best. You cared for the sovereignty of Graznia as I cared for Nicholas. And now they are both gone."

My eyes moist with tears, I chided myself for eavesdropping, and even more for being tearful at what I had heard.

"Where have you been?" demanded Jack, when I found him a moment later in the social hall. "Been looking all over for you. Tell me more about her, will you, Bobby?" Jack was plying little Bobby with chocolates and scribbling furiously in his ever present notebook.

Bobby examined a chocolate with the leisure of someone who knows there are plenty more. "I like the cherry cream ones," he said, and bit tentatively into the candy. "Well, she was ever so clever, knew lots of languages. But I thought she was silly, too. Always tucking people in."

I shuddered again at the thought of the assassin, striking as she played the role of the mothering woman.

"Mrs. Fitzhugh may not want Bobby interviewed," I said.

"Are you kidding?" Jack grinned. "The *Globe's* paying good money for this story. And Bobby and I are getting along just fine. Have another chocolate, son.'

I rummaged in my bag. "Bobby, here's something you lost." I handed him the stamp bearing the portrait of Ludovic of Graznia. "I thought I might ask you if I could keep it as a souvenir . . ."

"Sure, if you're a friend of Jack's here," said Bobby.

"Isn't the Order of the Silver Falcon enough?" Jack frowned.

"Jack makes wonderful boats," said Bobby. "Great big ones with sails. Right, Jack?"

"Say, Bobby," said Jack. "How about stepping outside for a minute? We'll pick this up later. Here, take the chocolates with you."

"Sure, Jack," said Bobby agreeably. "I'm going to be a reporter when I grow up," he said to me. I resisted the urge to wipe the chocolate from his face and hands. Without Fräulein Reiter, Bobby had begun to look quite disreputable.

"Lemme see that," said Jack. I handed him the stamp.

"Carrying a torch for the guy, huh?" he said sorrowfully.

"Well," I sighed. "Not everyone gets a chance to meet a handsome prince. And he is handsome. And charming in sort of a cavalier way. Must take generations of blue blood to develop that sort of casual arrogance."

"I see," said Jack.

"But that sort of thing is really kind of silly, isn't it? I mean, it's lovely to be nineteen and kiss a prince in the moonlight, but it doesn't have much to do with real life, does it?" I frowned. "Jack, he shouldn't have let Mr. Twist die for him. It was wrong."

"He kissed you in the moonlight?" exclaimed Jack. "What a story! 'Incognito Prince Kisses Daughter of Democracy Under North Atlantic Moon.' "

"Don't you ever stop?" I shouted. And wondered why I was angry.

Jack laughed. " 'Course, if *I* kissed you, it wouldn't be a story at all. But it'd be a hell of a kiss."

"Yeah?" I said.

"Yeah," he replied. And he kissed me. "You know, kid," he said. "I'm crazy about you."

"Oh, Jack," I said. "That's grand. I'm glad you didn't want King Ludovic to cut in."

Bobby Fitzhugh came rushing into the room. "Land," he cried. "Land!"

If you have enjoyed this book and would like to receive details of other Walker publications, please write to:

Mystery Editor
Walker and Company
720 Fifth Avenue
New York, New York 10019